Mandingo

By

Sidi

Published by

Harlem Book Center, Inc.
106 West 137th Street, Suite 5D
New York, NY 10030
Tel: +1/646-739-6166 or +1/646-739-6429

Warning!
This is work of fiction. All the characters, incidents and dialogues are the products of the author's imagination and are not to be construed as real. Any references or similarities to actual events, entities, real people, living or dead, or to real locales are intended to give the novel a sense of reality. Any similarity in other names, characters, entities, places and incidents is purely coincidental.

Cover Design/Graphics: www.mariondesigns.com
Photography: Alexei Production
Editor: Barbara Colasuonno

© Copyright 2006
ISBN 0-9763939-1-3

ACKNOWLEDGEMENTS

First of all, I'd like to thank Allah for allowing me to complete this project. To my beautiful family, thanks for being patient with me while my mind was concentrating on getting this novel done.

I am truly thankful to Roland. T Books vendor (Brooklyn Mall) for pushing me into a journey of writing books.

To my people running the book business in the streets, Omar Traore "Rubbish" from 125th Street, Tony Brown, Balde, Ishmael Sangnan, Massamba Amar Jamaica (Queens), Mustapha, Konate Moriba "le Gouru", Yigo Aboubacar, Abdou Boussou, Abo Ndiaye, 23th Street, 6Ave, Cheikhona Ba, 44th Street, Lex. And a special thanks to the two beautiful models, Sidibe Ibrahime "Papito" and Maimouna Ouedraogo "Mai La Princesse".

Special thanks to: J P Morgan Chase Bank-Harlem, Branch 61, Sean Burrows, Sarah, Jacinth Fairweather, Sharyn Peterson, Sharon Font, Sonya Merriel and Bonita Veal.

To my brother-in-law, Fadiga Aboubacar, Sidibe Hadja, Amy, Sidibe Zenab, and Aicha(Ohio) thank for support and believing in me.

Special thank to my friend, Hubert Daleba Gnolou. I know you been always there for me.

To my best friend, Meite Ibrahim Jean. Thank you for holding me down.

To my friends James W. Martin Jr. aka Jalike Ashanti Heru Herukhati, and Norma van Demark aka Ewunike Adesimbo.

Thanks to A & B and Culture Plus for their support and for believing in me.

To my partner Bakary Gasama (B.K), thank you for your support and encouragement.

Thanks to all of the readers who sampled the manuscript and gave me their feedback. There are too many of you to name individually, but you all know who you are, and I'm extremely grateful.

To my special friends from Sweden; Lisa Eriksson and and Haddy Sarr.

To my family Carlson (Bo, Inger, Jeanette and Angelica). Thank you for believing in me and stay up.

To one of my dearest brothers & friend, Sidibe Siaka, his wife, and two sons. I can't thank you enough for what you have done for me.

To my big brother, Ousmane Fofana "Restaurant bon appetit". Thank you for believing in me.

To my friend Marlon. L. 162+Jamaica do your thing.

To my friend from Burundi, Aimable Rulinda.

To Christine Jordan "28 Precinct Harlem". Thank you for keeping our community safe.

To Hakim bookstore, phone: 267-278-7888. I thank you for being there for me.

To my brother, Inza Sangare "Brikiki", and Kashan Robinson, best-selling author, of Veil of Friendship. Thank you so much for your support.

To my friends in Germany. Thank you so much for your support.

To my brother-in-law, Graig, and his beautiful wife, Corinne. Thank you for encouraging me.

To my man from Paris, Aaron Barrer, "le Congolais blanc". Grand merci. To my best friend, Ahmed Kaba "Bajo" le prince charmant de New York". Keep doing your thing.

To my body guard, Big Tony, and his family, and to many friends who helped. I cannot name you all but you know who you are. I do love, appreciate and thank you.

To my friend & partner, Raphael aka Pepe, Trazar Variety Book Store, 40 Hoyt Street, Brooklyn, NY. Thank you for your support.

And a special thanks to Kevin E. Young. If it weren't for you the project would not have been completed.

DEDICATION

I dedicate this book to
Jaqueline Carleson,
Sidibe Mamadi
and
Sidibe Mabana Hillary.
I truly love you.

PROLOGUE

Denise Jackson
January 2003

Although I'd been with boys before in high school, that's just what they were—boys. And none of them had the length and girth of the grown-ass man standing in front of me. I swear to God, he has to be longer than a ruler and wide enough to fuck up some of my internal shit. Still, I have to go through with this. That's the only way I'm gonna know if he'll be to women what I am to men—the best damned sex money can buy.

I'm scared to ask him to continue taking his clothes off. The bulge in his boxers is very impressive, and I'm afraid his dick is gonna spring out and knock me into the wall or something. To allay my fears, I try to concentrate on a different part by turning my attention to the rest of his body.

The muscles ripping out of his chest and arms make him look like a Mr. Universe contestant. Yet he's not so diesel that it's a turn-off. His six-pack stomach and his thighs are so lean and developed he could race against a horse. He's a strong stallion, alright. The stud-muffin every woman dreams about but never has the chance to experience. I'm about to audition him to make sure he's capable of making their wildest dreams come true. Well, at least those women who can afford him.

"Do you want me to take these off?" he asks in a heavily accented voice.

I feel the lump in my throat grow larger.

"Sure, sweetie," I answer as calmly as I can. "Where'd you say you were from? Africa?" I ask him even though I already know the answer.

"I am from the Mandingo tribe," he replies proudly.

"Nigga, you ain't never lied!"

As he pulls his boxers down, I see it's going to be worse than I thought. He's got a good twelve inches and he's only half hard.

Goddamn! I say to myself. *Some serious fucking is about to go down.*

PART ONE

Looking Back

Through the eyes of Mandingo, Denise, & Moriba
January 2003 to December 2002
Harlem, New York

CHAPTER ONE

Mandingo

As Denise steps out of her dress revealing a silky Victoria's Secret chemise, all my problems become irrelevant. All that matters to me are the ample breasts straining to stay inside her negligee. Her thighs are thicker than those of any of the pale faces that walk the halls of Columbia University and her butt is a sight for sore eyes. I look up into the air and thank Allah for also giving Denise the brains to make it into one of the toughest schools in America.

I've been lusting after Denise since she befriended me a year ago when I first arrived here. I guess the connection that blacks in America have with each other kicked in when she saw me. Back then, she didn't know I was African. I guess all she cared about was that I was one of the few dark faces in the lily-white crowd. I didn't care what the reason was, though. All that mattered to me was that she was the prettiest woman I'd ever seen in my life and she was talking to me. Just a few words and I was making plans for our wedding and honeymoon, especially our honeymoon.

Regrettably for me, I learned that there were a few problems with the plans I was making for Denise. First and foremost, she is what Americans call a carpet-muncher, meaning that she is attracted to other women. That difficulty alone loomed largely enough but, additionally, her occupation was another disqualifying factor. To put it bluntly, she was a high priced call girl, and I was a broke college student. We were definitely not a match made in heaven.

Even though Denise and I became close, I always beat her upside her head with questions about why with all that she had going for herself would she still decide to degrade herself by selling her body. She'd always say, "You're my boy but your broke-ass is just like all those other niggas trying to get some pussy for free." She had a point, but I still wasn't wrong. There are a million things a woman can do besides prostituting herself. All it takes is a little hard work.

Damn. Now I feel like a hypocrite. I'm talking all of that trash about Denise but the only reason she's about to give me some is because she wants to make sure I'll please the rich clients she has lined up for me. But hell, any excuse to be with this bombshell is good enough for me. She has a body like Vivica Fox and a face like Stacey Dash. Allah forgive me for the illicit acts I'm about to commit but I don't know a man who's strong enough to withstand her charms. I'm so glad Karen Steinberg told her about our little run-in.

Karen was a country girl from Kentucky who put the C, O, U, N, T, R, and Y in the word. I swear if you look in Webster's you'll see a picture of her smiling face right next to country. But I ain't mad at her though.

For one, she's one of the smartest people to ever graduate from high school in her state. How else do you think she got here? Poor white trash can't afford this place just like we can't.

The other reason I ain't mad at her is she looks like a blond- haired, blue-eyed Daisy Duke. Keep it real. Your eyes are glued to the TV, too, whenever you can catch the Dukes of Hazard reruns on Spike TV. What man wouldn't be lusting after Daisy Duke? Not to say that I was lusting after Karen Steinberg, but I noticed her.

Karen Steinberg has breasts similar to Denise's and long, flowing legs. She's pretty much the classic white bombshell. Kinda tall and slim with big titties. She does have a little phatty for a white girl. Yet, still, like I said, I wasn't all big on her. She stepped to me.

I was in the cafeteria one day when she came in. A couple of the resident loudmouths started talking trash to her after she grabbed her food so I motioned for her to sit with me. I guess I just felt bad for her. And I knew that the only reason they were clowning with her in the first place was because she wouldn't sleep with any of them. Nevertheless, I was certain that they would calm that shit down once she sat with me and I wasn't wrong. Soon as Karen Steinberg's ass hit the chair all of her hecklers became quiet as church mice. The resulting silence gave us the perfect opportunity to hold our own little private conversation.

Karen wanted to know what it was like in Africa. She asked if we still ran around hunting bears with spears. Although I thought that was an ignorant, racist question, I also found it amusing that those myths still exist.

I didn't answer her. Instead, I asked her if she still wrestled pigs in the slop pen. She started laughing. I guess she got my point because she changed the subject.

She asked me why blacks got mad about some myths and were quick to cling to others. Of course I didn't know what she meant so I asked her to be more specific. Her response made me fall out.

She said, "You got mad that I asked you if you were a hunter but if I had asked you if you had a big, African dick, instead, you would have been quick to agree with me."

After I finished laughing, I said, "That's because your first assumption was ridiculous and your second is true."

"Yeah, right," she said. "Everyone knows the myth about black guys being bigger than white guys. It's legend."

"Nah, baby girl, it's an actual fact," I said proudly.

"Well, show me," she replied.

"What? You can't be serious."

"I'm dead serious," she said, unaware that that was the beginning of the end for her.

We went back to my dorm room and I put on some reggae. I thought Shabba Ranks was appropriate for the moment.

I started gyrating my body to the rhythms of Shabba as I undressed. I could tell that she was more than impressed with my body. After watching her stare at my chest and arms, I decided to rub some baby oil on them to make them glisten. I planned to intensify whatever pleasure this naive white girl was feeling as she lusted over my African features. And, truth be told, she had no idea what the fact of my being of the Mandingo tribe meant. She was definitely about to find out.

When I finally got down to taking off my boxers she gasped. "Is that thing real?" she asked.

I grabbed her arm and pulled her to me.

"Come on over here, girl, and find out."

She started stroking my dick while she kissed my neck. I could feel myself starting to elongate. Soon I would be at my full fifteen inches.

I smiled when her kisses went from my chest to my stomach. She looked in amazement at my python and muttered repeatedly, "Oh my God."

"Don't pray to Jah now, baby girl," I said. "Your mouth got you into all of this trouble you're in."

I got tired of playing with Karen Steinberg so I finally grabbed the top of her shoulders and guided her down to her knees.

"So, what are you going to do with this big African dick?" I asked her. Without responding, she showed me.

Believe me when I tell you, the myth about white girls knowing how to suck a golf ball through a straw is not a lie. Come to think of it, a redneck, country-ass white girl has even more skills than a regular one. I didn't know that then, but I do now. But I'll tell you about that later. Let me get back to Karen Steinberg and her talented mouth.

At first, she kissed the tip. It was like a series of quick pecks on the lips. But instead of it being my lips, it was the round, sensitive head of my dick.

Out of nowhere, she glanced up at me with the most devilish grin I've ever seen then she took the plunge. She skillfully took me inside her mouth and wrapped her lips around my dick as if she was giving it a bear hug. All the while, she stared deeply into my eyes.

There's something about a woman looking in your eyes while she's pleasuring you orally. It's a reassurance that lets you know that she knows exactly what she's doing and who she's doing it to. And she was doing it to death.

She bobbed her head up and down as her mouth made slurping sounds each time she swished her tongue.

"Suck that big African dick!" I demanded, encouraging her.

I doubt that she needed my encouragement, though. She was already going to town.

When her oral prowess started to feel too good, I wanted her to stop. I wasn't going to let her get away with just a Lewinsky. I wanted to pound her white pussy for all it was worth, especially because of the dumb shit she said to me earlier.

"Are you ready for me to ruin that white hole?" I asked.

She started shaking her head and mumbling through slurps on my dick. Yet, that wasn't enough for me. I wanted to hear her speak in plain English.

I pulled my dick out of her mouth roughly and started smacking her in the face with it.

"Beat me with that black dick, Mandingo," she said while catching her breath. "Beat me with it."

I had never understood why my uncle Moriba cheated on his wives even though he had three of them and therefore shouldn't have been bored with any of them. But as I was severely degrading and disrespecting Karen Steinberg, the reasons started to become clear to me.

I would never be seriously involved with Karen Steinberg.

But she's a master at sucking dick so I wouldn't mind letting her do it to me again. I just didn't want her to feel like I thought she was special.

She had given me some oral sex that made me go berserk. And I was about to get some white pussy for the first time. I didn't care about Karen Steinberg so I told myself I could do whatever I wanted to her without explaining myself. She really didn't fucking matter to me then. So I fucked the shit out of her that day.

Karen Steinberg was every man's fantasy — a piece of ass you could do whatever the hell you wanted to with none of the bitching and moaning you usually had to deal with. She was the perfect "other woman" to me. She could have been any of the women my uncle Moriba cheated on his wife with. But that day, she was my first victim at Columbia.

After smacking her repeatedly in the face with my dick, I was finally ready to fuck her.

"Turn around," I yelled at her.

"You're too big for that way," she said with pleading eyes.

"I'm just a man about to prove that certain myths are not myths. Just turn the fuck around and take what I'm about to give to you."

Karen Steinberg remained on her knees while she turned around slowly…cautiously…deliberately.

I paused to stare briefly, somewhat in awe at how nice her ass was for a white girl, round and plump. It definitely wasn't a wide board butt like other white chicks. It poked out just the way I like it.

After putting on a Magnum condom, I nudged forward to tease her with the tip for a moment. She rocked back eagerly.

I knew that wouldn't last for long though. Her ass was about to run for the hills when I really started giving her the dick.

For fifteen minutes, I gave it to her an inch at a time. As every minute passed, I gave her another inch. By the time it reached ten minutes, she was ready to pass out. I was having none of that, though. I smacked her ass really hard until it turned red. I giggled to myself, pleased at how it wiggled like jelly. She looked back at me speechless. I could tell that she wanted to holler or scream or moan or at least tell me to stop smacking her ass so hard. My dick must have been killing her. Her breaths were caught somewhere in her throat. She wasn't able to make the minutest of sounds.

After I had made her take all of me, I started growing bored with the silence. I decided it was time to make Karen Steinberg get a sore throat.

I braced myself carefully behind her and grabbed her small waist tightly with both hands. I rammed myself into her as hard as I could. With each thrust I got more turned on by the way her ass was jiggling. Not to mention her whimpering had me really feeling myself. But it was still not enough.

I rocked back enough to totally remove myself from her then thrust myself back in. She let out a loud shriek.

At that point, I knew I had her where I wanted her so I started repeating the process of taking my dick out and thrusting it back in.

"Oh shit, Mandingo! Goddamn. Oh my damn. Fuck!"

Karen Steinberg was shouting out combinations of curse words I'd never heard before.

Yeah I thought, *I'm wearing her ass out.*

I had no idea about Karen Steinberg's previous sex partners. But I will say that she had one of the tightest pussies I ever had. At the time, I thought that she was so tight because white men have little dicks. My experiences with other white girls after Karen Steinberg clued me in that it wasn't true. It was just her. With that little-ass pussy, I must have been killing her.

I rammed my dick in and out of Karen Steinberg for about ten minutes until her shit started to get to me. Then I put the whole thing inside of her and started grinding it as deep as I could. If I remember correctly, I think I felt my dick hit her kneecap. I don't fucking know how and I know I didn't care. All that mattered to me at the time was that she had some good-ass pussy.

I can't even say that her shit was good for a white girl. She could have been red, black, green or orange, it didn't matter. Her shit was popping. It may have been the best shot in my life. That's why I kept fucking her even after that night. And I'm glad she wanted more. I thought it would just be one and done after I degraded her the way I did.

When I felt myself getting ready to come, I pulled out of Karen Steinberg and pulled the rubber off. She sighed as if she felt instant relief then I started smacking her in the face with my dick again. Eventually, I shoved it in her mouth and started barking out commands.

"Suck this big, black dick you white whore," I yelled at her. "Suck it," I repeated over and over as she obliged me.

After a couple of slurps from her talented mouth, I think I shot a gallon of come into her mouth while holding the back of her head to ensure that she didn't move. Once the last drop came out, I relaxed and slumped backwards.

She started gagging like a five hundred pound man was choking her with both hands. Then she ran to the sink and continued to gag while simultaneously spitting into the sink. Finally, she stomped over to me and preceded to tear me a new asshole.

"You have some fucking big-ass balls, you freakin' African," she screamed. "Some big-ass balls."

"What the fuck is wrong with you?" I asked, pretending to be totally oblivious to her issue.

"You fucking come in my mouth? That's what you do? You fucking come in my mouth?"

"What do you mean?" I said. "If you weren't cool with it, why the hell did you let me finish? You should have pulled away."

"No. You should have pulled away like any other man who had some fucking respect for me would have done."

"But you liked it…"

"I liked it?" she said interrupting me. "You think I fucking liked it?"

"Yeah. That's what white girls do. Black girls front like they don't like it, but white girls will gladly swallow your cum."

"Well, this one won't," she yelled, scurrying around look- ing for her clothes.

Once I realized she was serious, I apologized over and over. But she wasn't beat.

"No, you meant to disrespect me, Mandingo, so why should I accept your apology?"

"Because I really am sorry."

"You're not sorry. If you were sorry, why did you laugh at

me then?"

I'd almost forgotten that I had laughed. The whole situation was so fucking unexpected it caught me off guard. I didn't think she heard me. Still, I wasn't laughing at her. I was laughing at the situation. And even she had to admit it, it was a funny-ass situation.

Who starts gagging like that after you take your dick out of their mouth?

At any rate, I didn't tell her what I was thinking. She probably wouldn't have looked at things the same way as I did anyway.

Surprisingly, we were able to peace everything up that night. Or so I thought. To this day, Karen Steinberg stills mentions the time she says I disrespected her.

That night, though, after sulking for what seemed an eternity, she started complaining about not having an orgasm.

"How could you say that?" I asked. "You were screaming your fucking lungs out."

"I was screaming because I was in pain, you asshole, not because it felt good."

Karen Steinberg's words hit me like an unexpected sucker punch. But it wasn't because I was so big on her. I thought hard about what she said. Other women in my life had screamed like hell, too. I always thought that my dick was the bomb to them. But apparently I had the game totally fucked up.

"If I was hurting you, Karen, why didn't you say so?" I finally asked.

"Why should I?" she replied. "Your intention was to show me that black men have bigger dicks than white men and that you did. What reason did I have to just give up the fight before it even started?"

"All I know is that if someone is hurting you then you let them know. Hell, if it was a sister she would have said something," I said, trying more to convince myself than her.

"That's what you think, Mandingo, but you're wrong," she said sweetly. "Trust me, you're not just big because you're black. You're big for any man. And any woman who's had some of that big-ass dick was in pain. They were probably just too proud to tell you."

Out of nowhere Karen Steinberg started smiling.

"Correction. They probably didn't want to further inflate your already humongous ego."

"I'm not conceited."

"No one is saying you're conceited, but you do have a big-ass ego. Let a woman compliment you sometimes. You don't always have to give yourself props."

Clearly, my dick had Karen Steinberg talking crazy that night but her words did put a heart into what had previously just been some nice titties and a plump ass. Plus, I was still kinda upset about her not having an orgasm.

"Did I ever tell you that you're smart, Karen Steinberg?" I asked.

"I guess I should be worried," she said. "You're complimenting me. What the hell do you want?"

"Why do I have to want something?" I asked.

"Because men always do," she said. "They treat you like shit on a regular basis because they want something. Then they act like you're the fucking queen of England."

"Well, regardless if I want something or not, I've honestly always thought you were smart. Why else would you be here?"

Karen Steinberg never answered me. She just rested her head on my shoulders.

"I'm still turned on," she had said. "My pussy is sore as all hell, but I'm still turned on. Do you think you can finish the job without trying to kill me?"

Without answering, I pulled her over to me and started kissing her neck. Before long, I started hungrily sucking on her titties.

It's baffling to me why I hadn't touched her titties before despite being so big on them. I guess she was right about me not caring about her. I'm not sure I ever started caring. But I was sure that I didn't like the fact that she didn't come. I remember thinking that the only way I was leaving that night without her having an orgasm was in a body bag.

After sucking on her titties long enough to get hard again, I laid on top of her and eased myself into her. She wrapped her legs around my back and we started grinding together in rhythm.

"Yes, Mandingo," she moaned. "This is how you're supposed to give a girl some of this big-ass dick."

I have to admit, it felt a lot better doing it slowly and carefully than it did acting like I was running a hundred yard dash.

She let me lead for a while then she asked me to let her get on top. I didn't care. As long as she didn't ask me to stop. I was possessed by the thought of making her come wildly and crazily.

Wildly and crazily, it's funny I use those words. That's exactly how Karen Steinberg started acting.

When she got on top, she started grinding on me like she was riding a horse. It was kind of exotic. But it wasn't anything to write home bragging about. Then something changed. She started moaning really loud and hopping up and down harder and harder on my dick.

"Yes, Mandingo," she shouted. "Fuck me with this big black dick! Fuck the shit out of me you motherfucker!"

Karen Steinberg really started wilding out. She was bouncing on me like she was crazy. She grabbed a handful of my chest with her nails and was pounding me into the bed. It's a good thing I didn't have a girlfriend at the time or I would have been in trouble. I didn't care, though. The shit was starting to feel real good. And the way Karen Steinberg was acting was turning me the fuck on.

Before I had a chance to come the second time, Karen Steinberg let out a really loud shriek then slammed her pussy down hard on every inch of my dick. I could feel her pussy pulsating around my dick and before long she started to shake. Her eyes got really big and she became extremely quiet with the exception of her heart beating like an African drum.

She stayed that way for about three minutes then she lifted her head off of me and started kissing me on my neck and chest.

"Damn, this dick is good, Mandingo," she stammered. "Goddamn, this dick is good."

Before I knew what was happening, her mouth had found its way back down to my dick. She sucked it like I was about to give her a million dollars or something. Of course it didn't take long for me to get ready to bust.

When I felt it coming, I started pulling away. But she wouldn't let me.

"No!" she yelled. "I want to taste you this time. I don't want to waste a single drop."

I never told Karen Steinberg what I'm about to say. In fact, I've never told any woman what I learned that night. I found out that if you don't just try to go for yourself and actually keep the woman's enjoyment in mind then you will enjoy the sex just as much as she does, if not more. And she may let you get away with a few things she would have ordinarily freaked out about.

I can't believe she let me fuck her again after I came in her mouth. Then she let me come in her mouth again and swallowed it.

I have never been mad at Karen Steinberg since that day. Now, today, not only am I not mad at her but I love her. That's right—I love her. If you saw what I am seeing right now while Denise is undressing you would understand. I'm the luckiest man in the world right now because of a country-ass white girl named Karen Steinberg.

Like Don King says, "Only in America." Only in fucking America.

CHAPTER TWO

Denise Jackson

I've always loved my body but I became hyper aware of it the first time my mom's boyfriend had his way with me.

I was only thirteen at the time and an early bloomer. My mom cursed me out when I turned ten because she already had to buy me a training bra.

"I can tell that I'm gonna have problems with your fast ass," she used to say.

But I wasn't that big on boys. All I cared about was doing well in school so I wouldn't have to live the rest of my life poor the way I'd been living for as long as I remembered.

Anyway, my mom was working her dead-end job one night trying to collect overtime since her trifling-ass man had lost all of his money gambling again. Before she stomped out of the house, she told him that the least he could do was watch me when she went to work.

Up until that night, I had always loved how the rapist looked at me. My mom dressed me real corny-like every day in loose clothes that gave people the impression that I was either really fat or just funny shaped. No one ever saw that I was packing. Yet sometimes, when boys looked at me, I'd start singing the song Ed Lover and Dr. Dre made famous: "I'm naked underneath my clothes...I'm naked underneath my clothes."

I really didn't want to be with boys. But it was nice to get some attention every now and again. The only time I got attention at home was when the rapist chewed me up and spit me out with his eyes.

After my mom left, I went and put on my pink sweat-shorts. I used to stand in front of the mirror forever on Saturday mornings just to see how decent I looked in them. My ass was nice and plump and it always jiggled when I stood up on my toes.

If I could only wear some regular clothes, I'd be killing them in school, I used to say to myself.

I took my bra off and started rubbing on my breasts before I decided what shirt to wear. By then I was wearing a C cup, and I was mesmerized by how soft and perky they looked.

I pulled on a white undershirt and tied a knot in it just above my belly button. By then my nipples were hard and anyone would have been able to see my areolas through the thin white fabric. I wasn't wearing a bra.

Once I was convinced that the rapist would look at me the way I thought I needed him to at the time, I sashayed down-stairs and commenced my performance.

I ran to the refrigerator and held it open while I was fig-uring out what to do next. I wasn't certain until the rapist chided me. Then I knew.

"You know what your mom say about holding dat 'friger-ator open," he stammered.

Right on cue, I bent over and started fumbling around with some stuff on the bottom shelf. When he didn't continue protesting, I turned my head to see if he was watching me. Of course he was.

"Please don't tell my mom," I said innocently.

"You knows that I's ain't a tattle tale," he replied. "Plus, you and me can have secrets, right?"

Without answering, I just smiled and turned my head back towards the refrigerator, happy that I'd just gotten away with murder.

I felt good at that point but I wasn't satisfied. I got up and ran over to the sink and turned the water on really high. I can't tell you how many times my mom yelled at me in the rapist's presence about having the water on so high. But I was going for broke that night.

I grabbed a porcelain cup out of the dish rack even though my mom always demanded that I use plastic.

"My good cups are for company," she always said.

Nevertheless, I starting shaking the cup under the running water to rinse it out. Before long, I had made a mess. Water had splashed all over my shirt.

"Shit," I said, momentarily forgetting the rapist.

"What did you say, Denise?" he asked, sounding stunned.

"I'm sorry," I said, turning toward him. "I won't say it anymore. Please don't tell my mom."

"'member what I said, girl," he replied. "Secrets."

I could barely hear what he was saying since his com-ments were directed to the titties that were jiggling around under my soaked white undershirt. If the rapist had ever wondered before, this time nothing was left to his imagination. When I looked down, I could tell as much, and for the first time, I wasn't happy to be stared at.

"Let me go change my shirt," I said.

"What for?" he asked. "It is kinda hot anyways. Cool yaself off."

"No. I think I'd better change it. My mom would kill me anyway."

"I told 'ya, secrets," he said.

By then, I was scared. I remember shrugging my shoulders and slowly walking to the refrigerator after turning off the water and putting down the cup. I never even looked in it again. I just closed the door and crept toward the entranceway of the kitchen.

"Where ya gon', girl?" he asked, grabbing my arm.

"I need to go upstairs," I said fearfully.

"No. Stay here with me," he demanded, his eyes ogling me and his hands gripping me tighter. In fact, he was holding me so tight I had a bruise on my arm for several days afterwards.

"But I have to change. I just have to change."

By that time I was crying. I can never remember what he said to me after that. But what he did to me is forever etched in my mind, just as if it happened yesterday.

He grabbed at my breasts with one of his hands while holding me tight with his other. I cried violently and begged him to let go of me but he didn't. He continued to violate me by fondling me through my shirt until he finally just ripped it completely to shreds.

Once my naked breasts were revealed, he started sucking on them clumsily as if he was the thirteen-year-old virgin. At that point in my life I was clueless as to the right and wrong way to do what he was doing to me but I did know that he was hurting me. He was sucking on my titties so hard that my chest was purple, black and blue for close to two weeks after.

When he finally let go of my arm, the pain was so intense I couldn't even feel it anymore. I think it went numb. I started rubbing it to no avail until I had to use my hands to attempt to remove his hands from my ass.

Like a typical rapist, he had pulled himself really close to me so that I couldn't escape and palmed my ass through my favorite pink shorts with his nasty-ass hands. Before the night was over, he'd gotten so much filth on my shorts I never wore them again. Yet, at the time, I wasn't worried about my clothing. For good reason. I was worried about me.

I struggled with him meaninglessly as he pulled down my shorts. Once they were down, I regretted the fact that I hadn't pulled on a pair of panties. What I had always done to feel more comfortable was now just making things more convenient for the rapist. I was so frustrated with myself for being so stupid that I didn't know what to do.

When he started shoving his nasty hands up my virgin pride, I lost every ounce of fight.

"Stop. I'll let you do whatever you want but please wash your hands first," I begged him.

Surprisingly, he obliged by rushing over to the sink and washing his hands. Unfortunately, I was too shocked at that point to escape. I couldn't even scream. Hell, I didn't even whisper. I was stuck in a violent nightmare. Too bad I was wide awake.

I closed my eyes. It wasn't until he shoved his dripping wet fingers back inside of me that I realized that he was standing in front of me. He started kissing me all over with wet, sloppy, putrid kisses. If I'm remembering correctly, his breath made me throw up right in his face. But that didn't stop him. He was an old-ass fucking rapist who was overwhelmed with the idea of getting some young coochie. Not just any young coochie, though. He wanted my young coochie.

He took his belt off and unzipped his pants. When he pulled them down, I was appalled to see a shit streak running down the middle of his drawers. How could my mom stand to be with his filthy ass? His drawers practically stuck to his ass. I wouldn't have been surprised if some of his skin came off when he tugged his drawers down.

His was the first dick I had ever seen and it was the ugliest thing in the world. It was shriveled and old-looking. I didn't know it then but it was also little as shit. Well, thank God for small favors.

When his crusty little dick got his version of hard I knew there was no turning back. The rapist was about to have his way with me.

He turned me around and shoved himself inside of me without the slightest finesse or skill. Even though it didn't seem possible that his little-ass dick would hurt me, it did. I felt my hymen being ruptured. And when I looked down, specks of blood flecked my inner thighs. Not only did my arm and titties pulsate with pain, so did my girlish coochie. There was no question about it. I was definitely being raped.

I must have passed out but I don't remember for how long.

But I do remember that upon hearing a familiar voice, I was jerked back to reality.

"What the fuck is going on here?" my mom screamed.

"Mommy! He's raping me," I cried through my tears.

"Rape my ass!" he shouted. "Dat li'l bitch wanted it."

"You little whore!" my mom snapped at me.

She rushed across the kitchen and started smacking the shit out of me. My face, neck, head, back. Every inch of my body stung by the time she finished with me.

"Get dressed and get the fuck out of here, you nasty bitch," she sneered. "You need to get away from me for the night before I kill your hot ass."

I was shocked, stunned, violated, in pain both mentally and physically, totally defeated. I threw on the first thing that I could find and dragged my weary body out of the house. But before slumping down against the tree that was just outside our shack, I heard my mom say words that have never left me.

"I can't believe her hot ass would accuse you of molesting her," she said. "That hot little bitch better recognize that I don't put shit before my man."

I could not believe that my mom would put that dirty, smelly, broke, little dick, old-ass man before me, her own daughter. Yet as surprised as I was at the choice she made that night, I was floored by the decision she made the next day.

When I woke up on the grass, a police officer standing over me. I didn't know what time it was but there was a hint of daylight.

"What are you doing out here, little girl?" he asked me. "Where are your parents?"

"My mom put me out the house last night because...

because… because her boyfriend raped me and I told on him but she didn't believe me."

The cop looked me over carefully while trying to calm me down. By then I was crying hysterically.

Finally he asked, "Where do you live? I want to go straighten this out right now."

I was too upset to speak so I just pointed in the direction of our shack.

The cop grabbed my hand gently and walked me to our front door. He knocked repeatedly for about five minutes until we finally heard movement inside the house.

"Who the fuck is it at this time in the morning?" I heard my mom yell through the door.

"It's the police, ma'am," he replied. "Open up. I believe I have your daughter out here."

I heard my mom unlock the deadbolt and unlatch the chain locks. The door swung open violently. My mom stood there on the other side, jacked up and irritated. After all these years, I can't forget how betrayed I felt knowing that my mom fucked the rapist the same night he violated me.

"Ma'am, are you alone?" the officer asked her.

"I'm in my own house, minding my own fucking business," she snapped. "You said you came to drop my daughter off and you did, so peace out. I ain't trying to fucking kick it with you."

"Actually, ma'am, I need to know if you are alone because from the looks of your daughter, I have probable cause to believe that something unsavory happened to her. If the suspect is here, I need to question him."

My mom shot me a look that could have cut diamonds.

"That's your ass if your bullshit causes any trouble," my mom snapped at me. "Do you hear me? That' your fucking ass!"

"Ma'am, do you see your daughter?" the cop asked her. "Her physical condition is consistent with her recollection of the events of last night. Don't you see her bruises, ma'am?"

"I already told you that I ain't' trying to kick it with you." She turned to me before continuing. "I told you that no trouble better come out of this."

My mom started to walk away but the cop immediately stopped her. "Ma'am, you need to relax," he said. "I need to be aware of your whereabouts at all times."

My mom shot back, "How the fuck do you expect me to get somebody if I can't move freely in my own damned house?"

"You can move freely," he said reassuringly. "But I have to accompany you."

"Fuck this!" she spat before calling up the stairs to the rapist. "Come here for a second," she said once he responded. Again, she shot me the nastiest glance she could muster.

As soon as the rapist's foot came off of the last step, the cop gripped him and cuffed him.

"Ma'am, if you'd like to come to the station you can follow us," the cop said, "I need both of them in order to run some tests. If you choose not to come, an officer will bring your daughter back home as soon as we finish with her."

"Let me fucking tell you something," my mom screamed. "Don't you fucking bring her ass back here! She done fucked around and got my man in trouble... don't you bring her fucking ass back here!"

My mom slammed the door with the force of an earth-quake and never opened it up for me again. I'm not sure if she ever learned that the tests came back 100% conclusive that her man raped me. And God knows I don't know what happened to the rapist. All I'm sure about is that on that day an innocent thirteen year old grew up and began to fend for herself. I had to. I didn't have a choice.

I went through counseling for a little while after that and I know that I wasn't at fault for what happened. Yet I still blame myself. If I hadn't dressed so scantily in front of the rapist, maybe he wouldn't have been so tempted by me. Maybe everything would have been different.

But even though you can't change the past, the past can damn sure change you. That's why now, years later, I'm still funny about my body. Even in my line of work, I don't like people looking at me. In fact, I haven't been totally naked in front of anyone with the lights on since I was raped that day. Not until today. And even now, I'm crossing my arms, covering my breasts.

*****

"So, are we gonna do this?" Mandingo asks me. "Or have you changed your mind about putting me down with your program."

"I'm sorry, Mandingo," I said. "I was just haunted by a ghost from my past, that's all. I'm ready when you are."

CHAPTER THREE

Mandingo

Mandingo

Denise looks like she's an angel standing in front of me. But there has to be something devilish about a woman who does what she does for a living.

She's completely naked and I'm in absolute awe. Her titties are so plump and luscious. Her ass is amazing. And her face is a picture of perfection.

"Are you sure you want to do this?" I ask her.

"Your first lesson, Mandingo, is to never ask a woman if she's sure. You can't afford buyer's remorse. Once she's paid her money, just fuck the shit out of her and keep it moving."

"Is that what you want me to do to you?" I ask.

"What kind of question is that? How long have you been wanting this pussy?" she asks me with a smile. "Besides, I'd have thought you'd want to take your time with me and not rush things. You'll never have a piece of ass like this again."

"Is that right?"

"You had better know it, Mandingo," Denise says confidently.

By now, I've had enough. I can't wait another second to sample Denise. The funny thing is, though, she thinks she's sampling me.

Denise Jackson

I'm keeping my emotions under control despite my trip down memory lane and despite how my pussy started creaming after one look at Mandingo's tremendous dick.

Looking into his eyes, I know he wants me real bad. I probably want him a little more than that but he'll never know it.

"So, show me what you've got," I finally say.

Mandingo doesn't miss a beat. He walks, no struts, over to me. Gently, he takes my hand and leads me to the bed.

I'm amazed at the level of patience he exhibits despite the fact that he's wanted to bang me for as long as I've known him. I had expected him to pick me up and carry me to the bed. But he didn't. He's taking his time, exactly the way I would want a man to if I was into men, that is.

When we get to the bed, he gently eases me down and lifts my feet so I can slide back against the pillows. He takes one foot in his hand and massages it. Then he brings my toes to his mouth and starts sucking on them. I'm feeling so hot that I'm about to drown in my own juices. I can't wait to see what else he has in store for me.

He's totally into the realm of foreplay. After sucking my toes, he licks his way up around my ankles, then up my calves, then to the backs of my knees. Had I been standing, they would have buckled.

I'm moaning as he starts massaging the backs of my thighs while gently kissing the fronts. When he passes over my pussy to kiss and lick my ass, I'm little disappointed but not really. The things he's doing to me are very erotic. But still, I need something inside of me soon. And if it's not that big dick of his, it may as well be his tongue.

My entire body goes rigid when he surprises me by sticking his tongue in my asshole. The way he's moving it around makes me certain it isn't a mistake. I can't believe how turned on I am.

I'm thinking that I can't take another second of foreplay. He knows it, too. His tongue finally finds its way to my clot.

"Oh God, yes," I whisper to myself, trying to pretend that he's not getting to me.

Although my mind is trying to mask my pleasure, my body is having a hard time cooperating. Before long, he finds out one of the first reasons why all of my clients love to be with me. An eruption happens inside of my pussy and I start squirting rivers of my juices all over his face. He remains unphased. He laps them up like he's a dog dying of thirst.

Even though he isn't going anywhere, I grab a handful of his hair and pull him deeper into me. I grind my pussy so hard on his face that I'm not sure how he'll be able to breath. But I don't care. And like a trooper, he doesn't quit. He keeps pleasing me with his tongue until my whole body goes listless.

When I feel the tip of his big dick against the lips of my pussy, I immediately revive. I know I'm finally about to get what the fuck I've been waiting for.

Mandingo's dick stretches my pussy like it's never been stretched before. And his movements are totally in sync with mine.

I start grinding slowly as he slowly grinds into me. We both move in a slow circular motion. I love how he fills me completely.

There won't be any pussy farts tonight, I think to myself.

His hands are palming my ass cheeks like they are two melons, yet he isn't a brute with anything he does. He's really cognizant of the fact that I'm a woman and I'm delicate.

I can't decide which feels better, the way his yardstick fills me or the way his mouth sucks and licks my nipples. Whichever it is, I'm certain I don't want him to stop. Nor does he want to.

I remember that I'm trying to control myself so I beckon for Mandingo to let me get on top. He changes positions obediently.

I'm on top of him, hoping that I don't get too carried away. Yet as soon as I place him inside of me again, I realize how difficult that's going to be. I feel like a feen seconds after taking that first hit.

I lean almost completely back so I can get an extra couple of inches into the grind. I'm still calm, hoping he hasn't realized how much he's getting to me. I can't see myself holding it together for too much longer, though. He knows how to use his big thick dick. I am so doomed.

Mandingo

Denise feels so good to me right now that my life could end and I'll feel like I've experienced everything I need to experience.

I can't believe how juicy she is. She squirted so much shit on me, I can't imagine her having enough liquid left inside her body to keep her pussy as wet as it's staying.

I also don't understand how Denise is able to control her pussy so masterfully. She can't be too tiny since she's been selling her body for God knows how long. But, still, it feels unreal.

Either she's merely calm under pressure or I'm gonna have to work a lot harder than I planned to get to her. I was hoping she'd be jumping against the walls by now. Yet, she's a picture of calm. She has one hell of a poker face.

I remember the first time I saw Denise and started to have thoughts of marrying her, being with her until we grow old together. That would be so perfect. And our kids would be perfect, too.

I can't imagine two better-looking parents than Denise and I. If we had kids, their bodies would be flawless. I don't see an ounce of fat on her, and I'm sure there's very little on mine.

While I'm making plans for our future, Denise starts gyrating on top of me with more purpose than she had before. It feels like every muscle in her groin has decided to gather around my dick and squeeze as hard as possible. It's intense.

I remember thinking that Karen Steinberg was the best shot I ever had, but Denise has changed all that. She's so skilled at what she's doing and her body is so unreal. She's doing things I didn't think were possible. Just like that, she has me hooked. And I'm not even sure what the hell I'll be able to do about it.

Denise Jackson

I don't feel like controlling myself anymore. I want to take advantage of this good dick while I can.

Being with Mandingo is so different than being with the power brokers I service on a daily basis. Yes, their money is long as hell but I can't say the same thing for their dicks. All of them have pretty much left me unsatisfied. I've often wondered why I even waste my time.

I'm glad I finally listened to Karen. Mandingo is giving me exactly what I need so I'm one hundred percent sure I'm going to put him down with my program. He has all the material he needs to turn any woman out and then some. And he knows how to use it. He knows how to use it very well.

I've been trying to fill my mind with thoughts of business but I'm drifting into an unchartered land of ecstasy. I know now that I have to give in to what I'm feeling. I'll just have to let the chips fall where they may.

I start fucking Mandingo with abandon. I grind my pussy into him as if he's the last man on earth. And right now, he is the last man on earth.

"Yes, Mandingo," I shout out. "Fuck this pussy like you mean it. This dick is so fucking gooooooooood."

I'm mad at myself for letting the cat out of the bag but I

know I can't turn back now. Who gives a fuck if he knows I like his dick? I'm sure I'm getting to him as well. It's been so fucking long since I've had an orgasm with a dick, I have no intention of cheating myself out of one when it's in reach. My legs are starting to tremble already.

Mandingo

I'm glad that Denise is finally showing me signs of life. I thought my dick was just mundane to her but she's feeling it just like everybody else. She's feeling me just like I'm feeling her.

With that knowledge, I start moving faster under her, trying to keep up with her rhythm. I want us to be totally in sync with each other at all times. I'm not sure if it's possible but I want to take our satisfaction beyond where it is right now and maximize the pleasure we each receive. When I arch my back and lift my dick even higher up into her pulsating pussy, she notices it immediately.

"Yes, Mandingo, give me more of that dick," she screams. "Give me all of it."

I have no idea how I've lasted this long with her feeling so good but I know that I won't be able to keep it up for much longer. Every nerve in my body is at a heightened level of sensitivity.

Denise isn't making it any easier with the way she's gyrating on top of me. She also has me swimming in the juices that continue to pour out of her pussy. She's like a faucet. Her shit is definitely unreal.

Before either of us knows what's happening, we start to climax together. Denise lets out a howl similar to what a wolf would make and I start hollering like a bitch. I can't really explain what's happening with her pussy but it's tugging on my dick despite the fact that she isn't even moving.

I come for what seems like an eternity. With each jerk of my dick, Denise lets out another loud moan. I can't remember feeling this good before. Denise is everything I imagined she'd be and then some. All that I can do at this point is hope and pray that this isn't the last time I'll be with Denise. It can't be. I have to have her again. I don't know what I'll do with myself if I can't be with her again.

While I'm wondering what will happen next, I drift off to sleep. I'm not sure if Denise falls to sleep with me but I don't even care. I don't have the energy to try and wait her out. My body is too relaxed. For once in my life, a woman has given back to me all I gave to her and then some. For the first time in my life, I think I'm sprung.

Well, at least if I'm gonna be sprung it's with someone as banging as Denise, I tell myself. Yet I'm not sure if I'm awake or dreaming. I am sure, though, that just that quickly, Denise has wrapped me around her fingers. Now it will take everything in my power to pretend that I still have control, knowing that Denise has held every ounce of my resistance right between her legs.

CHAPTER FOUR

Mandingo

I woke up snuggled next to Denise, her body warm against mine, and felt happy for the first time in a long time.

Just over a year ago, my father had sent me to America to further my studies. He had saved his money as an elder tribesman for years exactly for that purpose. When I finished high school in Africa, all the dreams he had for me came to fruition. After being accepted at Columbia University, I moved to New York City and lived with my Uncle Moriba. All my father's dreams for me were finally coming true.

Everything was going perfectly for me until five months ago. My aunt answered a phone call and started screaming. I knew immediately that something was drastically wrong.

We learned that there was a political coup in my village and most of the elders, including my father, had been murdered. But that wasn't the worst of it. My entire family had also been murdered, and I was warned to never return to my village or the same would happen to me. I was devastated and clueless as to how I would survive in America without money.

Almost immediately after hearing the terrible news, Uncle Moriba started to treat me differently. When his brother was alive, he was so kind and nurturing. But after his death, Uncle Moriba started treating me like the redheaded stepchild. He went so far as to tell me that my father had paid for only my first year's tuition. I didn't know if he was lying or not but there was no one left to verify with. In a nutshell, I was fucked. I had no idea what I was going to do.

For a while, I started fucking up and lashing out at everybody. I skipped classes, cursed out my professors, and even got into scuffles with my classmates. I got so bad that the administrators at Columbia started calling me Mandingo The Troublemaker and threatened to have me expelled if I didn't get my shit together.

I felt it was too strong a line of action for them to even consider. They knew the hard times I was going through. If I had been born in America, everyone would have cared more about the murder of my entire family. But since I was an immigrant, they didn't give a shit about me or my people.

I knew I was running out of rope. But I couldn't control myself. I became more and more bitter and continuously acted out even though I knew what was at stake.

My one saving grace was Denise.

She was so supportive during those difficult times. She fed me every day, bought me clothes, and sometimes put cash money in my hands to make sure I was OK. And she promised that one way or another we would figure out a way for me to pay my tuition. I told her that she didn't have to do that. Yet I knew I had no suitable plan for my life. I was pretty much just passing time.

One night, Denise got a phone call that really upset her. I asked her what was wrong but she wouldn't tell me.

I assumed it had something to do with her hustle. She never liked talking to me about her business. Yet, she was doing too much for me to accept anything less but the truth. I bugged the shit out of her until she told me what had happened.

Apparently, a Dominican guy who worked for her showed up at one of her female client's houses and the woman wasn't satisfied by the guy. Supposedly, the woman was a player in the city's government and was extremely powerful and wealthy. Denise could not afford for someone like her to be unhappy.

So I asked her if there was anything I could do to help.

I'll tell you, if you don't know anything else, know to never offer your help unless you're prepared to do whatever it is they want you to do.

Denise knew from Karen Steinberg about my special attribute and that I would be suitable to satisfy her disgruntled clientele. Of course I had no idea what she was talking about and told her so.

"Come on, Mandingo! Grow up," she said. "Fuck the woman for me, just one time. She's rich as hell so it's not like you won't benefit from her pleasure."

"I'm happy with my fuck buddy, Karen," I said. "And what the hell do you mean that she mentioned my special attributes?"

"All she said is that you're packing," Denise replied. "You are packing, aren't you Mandingo?"

"That's for me to know and for you to find out," I answered.

"Boy, stop playing with me! You know you can't even afford to smell no pussy like this!" she said. "So listen. Help me out here and get some new ass in the process."

"So you're saying you want me to fuck some bitch for you? What do I get out of it?"

"Damn, Mandingo, you're gonna treat me like that?" she said, sounding stunned. "How soon we forget? Never mind. It's quite alright."

I could tell that she was mad so I tried everything to get back in her good graces. But it happened only when I agreed to do what she asked me to do.

In the end, it wasn't as bad as I thought it would be. The woman tipped me over a thousand dollars in addition to the thousand Denise paid me. I was rolling in the dough for a little while. But that was almost a month ago, and Denise has not asked me to help her out again. I guess she was feeling some type of way because of what I put her through before I agreed to do her the favor.

She probably would have never stepped to me on that tip if she hadn't gotten in the argument with Karen.

I learned that Denise was talking about how she had so many motherfuckers strung out, and Karen told her that she couldn't make me get sprung.

"You may end up saying ga ga, goo goo," Karen Steinberg said.

Before I knew what had happened, Denise approached me and asked if I wanted to stop playing around and make sure my tuition got paid. Of course I said yes.

She had one condition, though. She didn't want to go on Karen Steinberg's word alone. She needed to try me out for herself.

I may not be the brightest bulb on the tree, but I knew there was no way I was going to turn down her proposition or her condition, especially her condition.

Her condition was to make me promise that I wouldn't catch any feelings before anything popped off.

"I'm serious, Mandingo. You have to swear," she said. "You're my best friend and I don't want things to get awkward between us."

Not only did I swear, I pinkie swore. I've tried to be nonchalant since but deep down inside, I hoped that Denise would stop being so damned meticulous and just get down to business. I hated that about her sometimes. She had to plan everything. Whatever happened to spontaneity?

As I lay here looking at Denise, I realize that she may be one of the few people who truly cares about me. In addition to my three aunts, that is. And certainly much more than my Uncle Moriba, the polygamist, does.

My aunts names are Fateema, Mariam and Kadija, and they live in Harlem, the Bronx, and Queens respectively.

My aunt Fateema is the most attractive of the three. She's a tiny bombshell, only about five-three but totally stacked. She's about a hundred fifteen pounds, all in the right places.

Her breasts are humongous and she has a phatty, phatty for an ass. Her waist is virtually nonexistent and she has the tiniest feet.

Aunt Fateema's face reminds me of Iman. So, truthfully, I don't know how Uncle Moriba is able to pull her. His other two wives are cute, but she is on another level. If she was ten years younger, she'd be a woman I'd step to.

Aunt Mariam is a little taller, about five-five or five-six. She has ass for days and days and days. But she has nowhere near the titties Aunt Fateema has. And her stomach and waist are not as flat. Truthfully, she has a little pouch. But I don't think most men would mind. It probably flattens out when she's laying on her back.

Her most distinguishing feature is her voice. It's really high pitched and whiny and gets on my nerves. But for some strange reason, she doesn't realize how irritating it is because she talks and talks and talks as if she just loves the sound of it. I'm sure Uncle Moriba has told her, "Shut the fuck up," on more than one occasion. I don't agree with his leaving one wife to go to the next, but I can't blame him for wanting to get away from Aunt Mariam's loquaciousness. She drives me up the damned wall whenever I'm with her.

Aunt Kadija, on the other hand, speaks only one word for every fifty Aunt Mariam spits out. Aunt Kadija is quiet and I love it.

She's also tall, about five-nine, but far from lanky. She has a stunning shape. She looks like model material. She doesn't have big titties or a big ass. Everything on her body is perfectly proportioned.

Her face reminds me of Robin Givens. She's so about her complexion. And she's mad sexy. Yet, to me, a woman who doesn't run off at the mouth is sexy as hell. Aunt Kadija gets lots of points just for her quietness.

Between the three of them, my belly is always full. I mainly stay in Harlem with Aunt Fateema, but I plan things out so I'm always at the right house at the right time.

For instance, when Aunt Kadija makes her stewed chicken, I don't stop at any stop signs or red lights. I get my ass to her house as quickly as possible.

The same goes for Aunt Mariam when she makes her fish casserole. It's amazing. I never leave until the whole pan is gone and I've licked the plate. When I return to the dorm after her fish casserole, I have to lay down for hours until my stomach settles. I always feel like I'm about to burst afterwards.

I love my aunts' cooking but they take care of me in other ways, too. They wash and iron my clothes, give me money, and are always sticking up for me with Uncle Moriba.

When he says that I'm no good and can't do anything, they tell him that I will conquer the world. When he calls me stupid, they tell him how brilliant I am. When he says I'm a failure, they tell him how proud the entire family is over my accomplishments. I get all the emotional support I need from them. The only problem is that they are Uncle Moriba's wives. And I can't deal with them without dealing with him. So, many times, I avoid them and the things they do for me just to avoid my uncle. Seeing him takes all the joy out of my life.

CHAPTER FIVE

Moriba

My nephew, Mandingo, has had life handed to him on a silver platter just like my brother did. Neither of them has had to work hard for anything. I always despised my brother because of it and I despise his only living child. Neither one of them has any concept of actually working for getting what is needed in life.

I don't see how it's fair that I have struggled my whole life while my brother sat on his butt hardly doing anything. He did practically nothing in Africa then rubbed my face in it by sending Mandingo here for me to take care of. Sure, he sent a whole bunch of money. But what about me? That was the last straw. It was time for me to do something.

There's always some type of revolution going on in Africa. But many times, those trying to overthrow the authorities are defeated because they don't know enough. That was the case in my old village. They repeatedly tried to revolt but always came up short. So I helped them. I gave them information at my disposal. And they finally succeeded. In the end, my brother's silver platter was gone and I was left with the money he had given me for Mandingo. No way his son would see any of it. Never. Never in a million years.

*****

Yes, I helped with the revolt because of my hatred of my brother and his son. But that wasn't the only reason.

Fateema and I had been having problems for a while before Mandingo arrived. And truthfully, I believed she was about to leave me. But with Mandingo's money, I bought myself time by giving her more and more shit.

She came to believe that I was able to give her more because I was giving my other two wives less. I guess it made her feel more important. It made her feel like she was taking clothes off my other two wives' backs. But the truth of the matter was that I started spending Mandingo's money as soon as it arrived. Then because I didn't have enough money for him to finish all four years of university, I knew I would eventually have to either tell the truth about it to my brother or come up with some fantastic lie.

I chose to do neither. I decided to take care of two birds with one stone. I got rid of my brother and the need to explain. The spoils of war left me with all of my brother's money. And although things are still not perfect with Fateema and I, she's not going anywhere anytime soon. Flashing money in her face keeps her around.

That being said, I don't understand what Fateema's problem was in the first place. She was getting hers so I'm not sure why she had to get in my business and worry about what I was doing with my other two wives. Why should it matter to her what they were getting? It's not like she didn't know what was going on from the jump.

That's the problem with women. You can tell them some shit and they'll be like, "OK," but they'll still bitch about it later. I guess you can't win for losing.

If it's not one thing it's another with my wives. Fateema's always bitching about material shit. Kadija says that I don't spend enough time with her. And Mariam says that I don't really listen to her when she's talking.

You already know how I feel about Fateema and her gold digger shit. It's definitely not cool.

Maybe that's why I spend so much time with Kadija. She couldn't care less about the material things. As long as I'm up under her, she's cool. I should thank Jah for small favors. But she does stress me out when she talks about how another man would love to spend time with her if I can't. She may be right since she's fine as hell but what man wants to hear that? I'm doing the best I can so she should just be thankful for the moments I share with her.

On a similar note, Mariam should be happy I spend any time with her at all. That woman gives me a fucking headache. She talks and talks and talks, sometimes without even taking a breath. I think, *Damn...is she gonna choke or something or pass out?* She never does though. She talks your ear off until you ask her to stop. I don't know how she does it.

I guess I put up with her because she has a monster ass. I love doing it doggy style to Mariam just to look at her ass and think, *Yeah, all that ass is mine.*

Maybe that's why so many men are jealous of me. I'm the fucking man with my lineup of women. I have the model girl, Kadija, the round the way girl, Mariam, with the stupendous booty, and the bombshell, Fateema, who makes every other bitch feel inferior.

And since my brother is no longer alive, I've got all of Mandingo's money to boot. I guess I'm living the life. Like Don King says, 'Only in America.'

And I'm living the American dream.

*****

I love my life but I hate weekends and I hate holidays.

On the weekends, I'm always busy. I work late on Friday, too. I like to have sex with Mariam late Friday night when only a couple of hours remain in the day. I like to take her to the bedroom and bang her head into the bedpost as I hit on that ass doggy style.

But Kadija likes to be with me on Friday nights. She says that we should start off the weekend with who's most important to us.

I've tried to rationalize with her over and over. "Why see me for just a couple hours on Friday when you can spend the whole day with me on Saturday?" But she's still not beat. She wants what she wants and that puts a serious kink in my game.

On Fridays, I have to make sure I swing by the house in Harlem to pass off a couple of dollars to Fateema. Then after listening to Fateema bitch, I head over to see Kadija at my place in Queens.

On Saturday mornings, Kadija wakes me up to the best blow job on the face of the earth. I guess that's my reward for spending Friday nights with her. Then she feeds in bed. If I'm up for it, she gives me another blow job until I'm hard again, then she jumps on me and rides me like she's a Texas cowgirl.

After we both climax, usually together, she goes and gets a warm rag to wipe me off. Afterwards, I go back to sleep and she goes downstairs to eat breakfast by herself at the kitchen table.

Saturday mornings are the most peaceful moments in my week. Kadija knows how to take care of me. She knows how to speak when spoken to and not bother me when I'm trying to relax for a minute. As long as I'm in the house with her, she chills. She doesn't bother me. Yet she caters to me like a good woman's supposed to.

I've wondered over and over why I don't just be with her. She's pretty enough and she soothes me. But one woman is not enough for me. Variety is the spice of life, and I'm spicy as hell. If I was only with her, I would miss out on all the good things my other wives have to offer.

Case in point — Fateema's sex. For the last year and a half, since our problems before Mandingo arrived started, we would only have sex on Saturday night. But if you've ever been with Fateema, you'd understand why I'd accept whatever she gave me whenever she wanted to give it to me.

I used to be as big on Fateema as I am on Kadija. We used to spend a lot of time together and did many things that I've never done with Kadija or Mariam. We went to plays, museums and art galleries. We pretty much have seen the best of everything New York City has to offer.

But Fateema's biggest asset is also her biggest curse. Fateema has the tiniest pussy ever created. I deal with it but I have to deal with her first. She always says, "My pussy is tiny as hell and I plan to keep it that way."

What Fateema means is that she doesn't want to have any children.

I used to be head over heals in love with her but her decision to not have children is a deal breaker. The only reason I accept it is because I know I can have more than one wife, maybe not legally in America, but all my wives understand.

I'm selfish. I always put myself first. I'm not going to give all of my money to no crumb snatcher right now. Eventually, I'll think about leaving a legacy. But since that's not an option with Fateema, I can't allow myself to get too caught up. I just enjoy what I have and take things for what they are.

What do I have, you may ask? I have Fateema and the best damned sex Mandingo's money can buy. And believe me, her shit is the best. That's why I'm not ashamed to say that I'm turned the fuck out. She has me sprung in the worst way. I'm whipped beyond belief. So for a weekly hit of her tiny pussy, I give her whatever she wants.

I remember the first time I was with her. After I finished sucking on her titties and squeezing her ass, I didn't think things could possibly get any better. But they did.

I kissed on her clit softly until she started shivering. Then I opened up her lips so I could taste all of her sweet pussy. I took in all of her wetness. And, goddamn, it was good to the last drop.

Then I noticed how small her pussy was. And it was so

pink. It's smallness was in perfect contrast to her thick, pulsating clitoris. I sucked and licked and kissed my way into total ecstasy. And on the way, I took her ass right along with me.

That's what I do with her every Saturday evening after spending a good part of the day with Kadija. I rush over to Fateema and get caught up in her pussy. Once I'm totally spent, I head to my house in the Bronx so I can chill with Mariam for a couple of hours before it's time to go to sleep.

If I'm lucky, she won't talk me to death and give me a fucking headache before the night's over. If I'm really lucky, she'll give me one of her off-the-meter dick suckings. Yet, when she does it, she expects to get her shit off too. And I don't have a problem fucking the shit out of her because her big, fat ass is legendary. Sometimes, though, I can barely breath after I finish getting it on with Fateema. Still, on nights when I feel like I'm gonna have to fuck her and not just get a licking, I drink a bottle of China Man Ginseng, pop a Viagra, and wash it down with a can of Red Bull. I need a set of wings to fuck Mariam after being worn out by Fateema.

One thing I can't front on Mariam about, though, is how she never hesitates letting me give her crazy back shots after she slobbers all over my dick. She rams her tiny butt hole back into my dick like a true champion. On nights like that, it doesn't matter how worn down and exhausted I am. I always find a way to catch my second wind.

Both Kadija and Fateema suck my dick haphazardly, never with the care that Mariam puts into it. But they both still do it pretty much every time we fuck. Trying to get either of them to give me their assholes is a different story. It's always a treat when I have enough energy to give Mariam back shots. Sometimes, I wake up Sunday morning wanting a second dose of her asshole despite knowing that I have to rush back to Kadija so she and I can either go to the mosque or eat breakfast together. There's something about a woman who allows you to treat her like a freaky bitch in the bedroom that makes a man feel like a bigger man, especially if she's your wife and not a piece on the side.

Speaking of Kadija and Sundays, though, I don't understand what her problem is when I arrive an hour or two late. She complains because she wants breakfast. It shouldn't matter if she eats at a breakfast place or if she eats at a lunch place. But she has a thing about breakfast and I think it's because she knows I'm not that big on it. I don't know what it is about women but they always seem to be happiest when you do something for them that is totally for them, something you don't enjoy all that much. It's too much for both of us to be happy. So she bitches and moans if I'm not eating an omelet even though she knows damned well that I'd rather be eating a cheeseburger or a fried fish sandwich.

It's hard work being a man, especially holding down three complaining asses.

But I wouldn't have it any other way. I like the variety of pussy. I get to ride around town sporting whichever wife I feel like being bothered with at the time. And when any of them gets on my nerves, I'm able to move on to the next.

For this reason, other men smile in my face but talk shit about me behind my back. They wish they could have my life but they can't. It's hard work being the motherfucking man but somebody's got to do it. It may as well be me.

Thanks, Mandingo. Your money helps me to be the man a whole lot easier.

CHAPTER SEVEN

Denise

After fucking Mandingo, I was convinced that with a dick like his there's no reason he shouldn't be the man. He should be making money hand over fist. But he isn't right now. He's just a broke-ass college student. We are gonna do something about that. I have a plan. That big dick nigga is gonna be paid in full. And with my percentage, I'll be more than alright. Money, money, money… MONEY.

*****

Mandingo is a dangerous combination — a cute nigga with a big-ass dick. But he lacks the hustler mentality he needs to take advantage of his shit. It's such a shame what happened to his family because he needs someone looking out for his ass. He's mad childish.

I'm at a soul food joint on 125th and Frederick Douglas about to feed his broke ass while we discuss the business of putting money in his pocket. Yet, even though this is his favorite spot to eat, he's late as hell.

I'm constantly telling Mandingo that time is money. But he just doesn't understand the proverbial statement, 'The early bird catches the worm.' The nigga is always somewhere sleeping while the rest of the world is out there grinding on some type of paper chase.

*****

While I'm waiting for Mandingo, I search through my IPOD to see which chicks on my "burnt out bitch" list Mandingo can bring back to life.

I used to think that my Spanish escort, Manuel, was packing until I slept with Mandingo. Manuel does have a nice size package but he's had his problems. His exact words: "Her shit is so ran-through that I could barely get my dick to touch one wall. I know I'm not small so I can imagine how a little-dick dude would feel fucking with her."

Whenever he put a woman on blast like that, I put her on my "burnt out bitch" list. I can only imagine how one of them would feel if they saw their name on my list! But shit, they probably wouldn't even care as long as they got some good-ass dick.

Being a burnt out bitch means they know they're burnt out. And they're cool with it as long as no one ridicules them.

I have the remedy, though. Mandingo. He'll fill up every inch of their worn out holes. I'm about to make them actually enjoy sex again. But still, I wonder how they got to be that way in the first place.

After my mom put me out, I was forced to survive on the mean streets of New York. And I can't front, I had to fuck more than my fair share of niggas just to put clothes on my back and food in my stomach. But some bitches fuck just for the sake of fucking. Those are the ones with pussies that are all beat the fuck up. A bitch like that would never get a licking from me. You won't find me asphyxiated and dead because my head got stuck inside of some stretched out bitch's pussy. Hell, no! I'd give her a look and walk out of the room no matter how horny I was or how much money was on the table. There's no way I'm putting my lips on some shit that I know has seen too many faces and been too many places. It's better to accept the fact that all money ain't good money and leave with my pride and dignity intact.

*****

Mandingo walks in and makes me lose my chain of thought. There's something about seeing a nigga right after he's just beat your pussy up real proper-like. You can try to play it cool but you know damned well that you want to jump in that nigga's arms and start in with him all over again. But a bitch can't play herself out. I have to maintain control at all times. Besides, I'm a pussy-licking bitch. I'm not supposed to be feeling some type of way about a dick.

"See, this is what the fuck I'm talking about! You can never just be where the hell you're supposed to be when you're supposed to be there!" I cut his ass off at the pass before he has a chance to try and charm me. "You're making me think you'd fuck up my money already and I haven't even put you down with my program yet."

"And it's nice to see you too, Denise. I guess it means you liked the dick. You told me you weren't gonna put me down unless you sampled me and determined that I could hold my own." He reached around and started patting his own back. I hated him for being so right.

"Don't break fly with me, nigga. So what? You have the material to work with. But that don't mean you know how to use it." I'm lying my ass off. "You act like you got a bitch sprung or something." God knows that if I wasn't always so careful not to catch feelings, I would.

"Whatever. Did you fix a plate for me?"

If looks could kill, he'd be dead for saying some dumb shit like that.

"Yeah right, motherfucker. I'm gonna pay for your shit and prepare it for you, too? You must have bumped your motherfucking head."

He starts doing the "Gator" dance from Jungle Fever, trying to make me laugh.

"Denise, please. Can a nigga get a couple of dollars to get something to eat?" He keeps dancing. "My stomach is growling and I need to eat, eat, eat."

He's a stupid motherfucker.

I hand him a twenty and he dances away. I start dripping just looking at his nice ass.

*****

As Mandingo eats his food, I can't front, I'm going through it. Every time he puts something in his mouth to chew, I have to force myself not to swoon.

Just watching him suck on a bone and licking the juice off the side of his bowl of peach cobbler gets me going.

I'm having some serious issues right now. I have to come up with a way to cool my hot ass down.

"Umm, Mandingo." I decide to catch the nigga off guard and come at him in a way in which I can save face. "I wasn't lying when I said that there are a couple of things you could do better. I mean, you have a nice dick and all, but once I show you how to work it more effectively, we can really make some money. I'm gonna have to help you from time to time to keep you on point. But before I put you out there, I definitely need to work with you."

Yeah. I'm about to get more of that good dick.

"That's cool. Whatever I have to do. I'm tired of being broke. I'm not used to this shit."

I hate that he's being so nonchalant.

*****

It was torture waiting for Mandingo to finish eating. But I'm happy now. We're driving in my Benz about to go to my place and get it the fuck on. My pussy is pulsating already.

*****

I don't even park as carefully as I normally do when I get to my place. I don't have time for fun and games right now.

I walk in the door with Mandingo closely trailing me. As soon as I punch in the code to disarm the alarm, I get right to it.

I grip Mandingo up and start kissing him while I rub on his chest.

"This is how some women like their shit. It's all about passion. Look into a woman's eyes and see that she needs it right then and right there."

"It is?"

"Shhh!" I cut him off really fast. I don't want him to say any dumb shit that gets me out of the mood.

I can't tell you how many times men whined and moaned and threw money at me just to get me to suck their dicks. I've fucked for money but don't try and make me suck their nasty dicks. Most of the time, it's no dice.

I can honestly say that in over five years, I've only sucked three dicks. But I had to. For whatever reason on those nights, I didn't feel like turning down the money.

But this night, as I pull Mandingo's pants down and kneel in front of him, I'm not asking for a dime because by the end of it, I know I'm gonna feel like a rich bitch anyway.

I start sucking his dick like a trooper, making sure he's up to the task of taking me to cloud nine.

"Goddamn, Denise. That feels so fucking good."

His words of encouragement sound good but I don't need them. I'm too turned on by the fact that I'm about to get what the fuck I've been wanting all afternoon.

"Put your tongue down my fucking throat, Mandingo," I tell him when I get up. I try to swallow it, too, since it gave me so much pleasure before, but there won't be time for that tonight. I need the dick. I need the dick. I need the dick.

Almost on cue, Mandingo gets down on his knees and

tries to return the favor.

"No. I don't want that. Not tonight. Tonight I want you to just fuck the shit out of me."

With one swoop, Mandingo lifts me up and carries me to my bedroom. He drops me on the bed with so little care that I finally start to feel like he's getting where I'm coming from. He does.

As he roughly pulls of my clothes, I get hornier and hornier. The beast in him is releasing the beast in me. And I'm ready to growl. And I probably will as soon as he puts that big dick in me.

He finally gets me naked so I give him more instructions.

"Don't play with me tonight, nigga. Fuck this pussy right. Fuck me hard. Trust me, you can't hurt me. So fuck this pussy hard."

Mandingo shoves his dick in me and I gasp. I'm finally getting what I need.

He's on top of me in a push-up position and every muscle in his highly toned body is flexing. While his dick is working this pussy out, his body is working out as well. And his heavy breathing lets me know that he's also getting in his cardio. And besides all that, his dick is doing wonders for my pussy.

"Yeah, Mandingo, that's right. Don't play with this pussy. Fuck this pussy. Give me that big, black dick. Give me that motherfucking dick."

I don't mean to but I tear up. At first it's barely noticeable but soon the tears flow freely.

I can't believe this motherfucker is seeing that his dick has brought me to tears.

"Yes, Mandingo, yes. Give it to me." I choke out. "Give it

to me. Give mommy that dick, poppy. Give mommy that dick."

*****

I come hard and fast and so does Mandingo right along with me. I was so out of my mind that I forgot to make the nigga put on a condom. His little men shoot up far inside of me when his dick starts jerking.

"Now that's how you fuck a bitch, Mandingo. That's how you fuck a bitch."

*****

I wake up and Mandingo is asleep next to me, snuggling against my back, his arms wrapped around me. I feel so safe and secure. Yet I know I can't enjoy the shit for too long despite the fact that it just feels right. I need to do damage control and I need to do it right away. I can't have the help feeling like they can make the boss do whatever they want her to do.

I nudge Mandingo hard. He doesn't move. So I push him really, really hard.

"Get up, Mandingo! Damn!"

He wrestles himself awake.

"What's up, Denise?"

"Get that ass up, that's what's up. I didn't say your ass was gonna stay here. I said I wanted to teach you some shit. Now that the lesson's over, your ass has gotta go."

"Come on with the bullshit, Denise. You know your ass wasn't trying to show me shit."

"Can you stop back talking me, nigga? Don't you know that in the corporate world that's called insubordination?"

I can see he's offended so I back off a little.

"Listen, Mandingo, I know Karen told you that shit about being slow and delicate which is the right way a lot of the time. For some women it's right most of the time. But you have to learn how to switch your game up. Sometimes a woman just wants to be fucked. I wanted to show you how a woman acts at times like that."

"So I guess those were fake tears I saw?"

"No, nigga, those tears were realer than real. I guess I could say that they were the realest. But what did I tell you before any of this started? I like the dick. But I was having a moment. You promised me that you wouldn't get caught up and all emotional and shit. We need to handle our business together and I can't have you catching feelings after only the second time we've fucked."

"So you're saying that this won't be the last time?"

"Far from it. But you can't scare me into making it the last time. I like your dick just like I'm sure you like my pussy. But you have to maintain, Mandingo. Don't go getting all bitchy on me."

"I feel you."

I don't believe him but I did save face. I accomplished just what I set out to do — damage control. Game, set and match, Denise.

CHAPTER EIGHT

Mandingo

"So what do you want me to do? You want me to wait for you on the couch while you get yourself together to take me home?"

"Take you home," Denise snaps. "You're a grown-ass man! Why the fuck would I have to take you home?" She reaches across the nightstand and grabs her purse. "Here, nigga. Here's fifty bucks. Take a gypsy cab." She peels off more money. "And take this couple of hundred as a tip for being so studious in your lesson. You did this pussy some justice."

Denise falls asleep not a minute after she gives me the money. I feel so played.

I guess it's not a love connection. With her everything is business.

*****

Denise has my head going through so many changes I don't know what to do. I'm in a quandary of sorts.

I appreciate the fact that she's like my big sister and is teaching me much needed lessons about life. But at the same time she seems so cold. How does a person get like that?

I know about the rape. I know about all the fucking and sucking she's had to do to survive. But still, shouldn't we always maintain a positive attitude?

Maybe I'm just tripping. Maybe I'm just mad that I'm sprung on her and she's not sprung on me. And that's a terrible fucking predicament to be in.

Denise

I'm glad Mandingo's sprung out over this pussy because I'm so sprung out over his dick. But it's not just the dick. It's him. I'm glad I was able to play the shit off, though. A bitch ain't trying to be hurt. This shit is happening so fast. And the last thing I want is to lose my best friend. I wonder if I made a mistake getting him hooked up in all this shit.

Mandingo

I'm wondering if I made a mistake getting hooked up in Denise's lifestyle.

I'm not upset, though, that I was able to fuck her, twice. And she told me that she's definitely gonna fuck me again. That should make me happy as hell. But it doesn't.

Denise means more to me than just a piece of ass. There's always Karen Steinberg if that's what I need. Denise is my peoples. She's my heart. I care more about her than I care about anybody. I would never do anything to hurt her. But to her, I'm just a dick and a dollar sign. I never thought that it would be possible for me to be played like this.

*****

Given how I'm feeling, I decide to go to a graveyard. I know that a graveyard here won't have my family, but I feel an intense need to show my respects and a random graveyard is all I have right now.

I pick a tombstone and immediately strike up a conversation with my dad. I miss him so much.

I hear his spirit telling me to relax, that everything will be OK, that everything will work out in time.

"Just stay strong," he always said. "Look to Jah and Jah will guide you. Don't only rely on your own faculties."

I'm wondering if that's what I'm doing by deciding to be a male hooker. I know Denise calls it this big, respectful name and paints an exotic and classy picture of it. But at the end of the day, all I'll be is a male hooker. I don't know if I can deal with that. Money is fine, but I'm not trying to sell my soul. I do still have my dignity. And I'm not selling that away to nobody, no matter how much I'm paid.

*****

"Mandingo, I need you to come over right away."

Denise's voice sends chills up my spine.

"I have an important client for you to take care of. And believe me, once you've finished with her, I swear you won't have to worry about your tuition ever again. This bitch is rich and talkative. She's just the type of person you need. All her friends and associates are rich too."

*****

Just that quickly, all of my tough talk and moral pronouncements go out the window. I see an opportunity to come up financially, and I'm ready to grab it as quickly as the words leave Denise's mouth.

*****

I'm told I have to go to Long Island to meet with the wife of a real estate developer. Her name is Chemise Goutier. To me, her name even sounds like money. I'm just hoping she turns out to be cute.

Since I'm broke, Denise uses her credit card to rent a car for me. It's nothing spectacular, just a Ford Taurus. But, still, it feels good to have wheels for a couple of days.

After exiting the Long Island Expressway, I follow the directions Denise gave me and watch as the scenery goes from worst to first.

When I find Chemise Goutier's house, I turn onto a road which is really a long driveway and park in massive parking lot. The multi-million dollar house is set far back from the lot. I walk up a long stone path to her front door and ring the bell as casually as I can. A stunning woman opens the huge front door. I'm amazed.

Chemise Goutier is breathtaking. She's an older white woman but as classy and fine as Tina Turner. Her ass looks firm for her age and her legs and tits are real nice. She has stunningly beautiful face.

And she's about to pay me for some dick.

This business may not be as bad as I think.

*****

I get a tour of the house but it's actually more like a mansion.

She starts with the living room which is outfitted with a bar along one entire side of the room. I've never seen so much expensive shit in my life. Hennessy, Crown Royal, Remy Martin, Jack Daniels, Patron, Amadale, Grey Goose, Absolut, anything and everything.

At the far end of the bar is a walk-in refrigerator. In there, I spot hundreds of bottles of Moet, Dom Perignon and Crystal.

These motherfuckers must have some real serious cake.

"OK, darling," she says in a sophisticated voice after taking a sip of her drink. "You've seen enough down here. Let me take you upstairs."

With a devilish look on her face, she puts her drink down on the polished mahogany bar and takes my hand.

I'm anxious to see and hear how a woman with so much class acts when she's getting some real serious dick.

She leads me up the winding staircase. I make sure to step delicately on the plush rug. I wouldn't be able to afford to replace it if I fucked her every day for a year straight.

Small lights are embedded in the treads all the way up the stairs. I guess Mr. Goutier wants to make sure no one falls and blames it on bad lighting.

Mrs. Goutier is starting to get anxious because she cuts short the tour and takes me directly to the bedroom.

Let me tell you about the bedroom. It's as big as my uncle's entire first floor. There are built-in shelves throughout the room with sweaters and other things tucked neatly in them.

On one wall, there's a high density big screen television, probably about sixty inches wide.

The bed is tremendous. It's like a king and queen combined into one so I know it was custom made. It has a canopy with extra oak support rails and exotic silk curtains hang from it.

Above the bed on the ceiling are several huge mirrors. I guess Mrs. Goutier uses them to help elevate her passion when getting her freak on. The set-up is perfect for some real serious fucking.

As impressed as I was when I first saw Mrs. Goutier, I'm more than impressed as she starts taking off her clothes.

Goddamn! This white bitch is stacked.

Her titties must be a thirty-six double D and her stomach is flawless, no bulge and no wrinkles.

Below her stomach is a perfectly manicured pubic region and some really thick-ass thighs.

Her ass is fat as hell and it's not wide like most white women's asses. It pokes out like a sister's would. I wonder to myself what the fuck is wrong with her husband. I'd be slinging dick to her every chance I got. This bitch is holding it down as good as any sister I've ever seen.

She sees the way I'm looking at her so she addresses my eyes.

"I'm passing," she says.

"What?" I don't know what the fuck she's talking about.

"You're too young to know what it means. Ah, well, maybe you've heard stories before about black people so light skinned that they pass for white. Well, I'm one of them. And don't try to judge me. My life's been a whole lot easier as a white woman than it would ever have been as a black woman. My husband's sitting on nine figures, quickly approaching ten. And I have access to all of his money."

I couldn't care less about her passing or anything else in her personal life. All I want at this point is to fuck the shit out of her.

"So, because you're passing does that mean you won't really know how to suck this dick real freaky-like?" I pull it out.

"Oh, honey, don't worry about me. I've been around the block a couple of times as both a black woman and as a white one."

She walks over to me erotically and stoops right in front of me. I feel mad conceited because this classy old bitch is bowing down right in front of me on her knees just like any slut from the Bronx or Brooklyn would do. I'm getting a nine-hundred million dollar dick suck. I know now that I am the motherfucking man. I know that I'm about to be richer than a motherfucker.

Mrs. Goutier is sucking my dick so good it makes me feel

more at ease. I'm getting beyond relaxed.

"Yeah. Suck that motherfucking dick," I urge her on.

"I love it when you talk to me like that, daddy."

Shit. I ain't said nothing but a fucking word.

"Suck this big black dick, you nasty slut. Suck it, you whore."

With every degrading word I say, Chemise gets more and more turned on and I become more and more comfortable. I had started out wanting some of Mrs. Goutier's pussy bad as hell, and now I'm about to fuck the shit out of her.

I eat her pussy the way Karen Steinberg showed me. Then I mix in some of the rough shit Denise showed me the other night. Chemise is feeling all of my skills and my package. Well, the dick already speaks for itself. I ain't got to say shit about that.

*****

When I finally put my dick inside of Chemise she lets out a yelp. I can tell she isn't ready for all of it. But she doesn't back down. To the contrary, she surprises the fuck out of me.

"Yeah, you black motherfucker. Give me that big black African dick. Fuck me, you African black bastard. Fuck the shit out of me with that dick. Come on, you pussy! Fuck me!"

All her class goes right out the window. Chemise is in the mood to get fucked like a dog.

And that I'm doing, and doing, and doing. And all the while I'm wondering when I'm gonna tire this bitch the fuck out.

At least by now her pussy should be sore as hell.

Chemise doesn't relent, though. I swear, I've been fucking this bitch nonstop for an hour and a half. And I've been fucking her hard. Still she keeps taking everything I have to give her and then some. This bitch has definitely had some experience with hardcore fucking.

"Chemise, don't you want to get on top?"

"No. I'm loving the way your ass muscles flex when you ram that dick inside of me."

I glance behind me and notice that's she's caught up in the image in the mirrors.

"Well, will you be able to see if I do it doggy style? I want to see that big ass."

"Sure. I'll let you have some fun, too. But I want to get back to the missionary position before we come. I want to see how you jerk when you come in this good pussy."

It's funny how much confidence we have in ourselves. I'm not going to say that Chemise had some bad pussy but it wasn't Denise's. It wasn't even Karen Steinberg's. I mean, it's been over an hour and a half and I still haven't nutted. That has to mean something.

But I can't front on her body, though. Her ass is jiggling like a bowl of Jell-O. And it's softer than a motherfucker. Plus her face is pretty as hell right now looking past me up at the mirrors. This is a banging-ass bitch.

Yet I can see why she needs to fuck a nigga like me. I can tell that's she's been around the block a time or two. Her pussy doesn't feel as snug as Karen Steinberg's or Denise's. Yeah, I'm still able to fill up her hole. A little dick nigga can't do shit for Chemise. She must give her lily white tiny wee-wee husband a heart attack every time. He'd probably be better off just eating her pussy and calling it a day.

I never understood why so many white men on the internet have ads out looking for black men to fuck their women. But now I do. Fucking a chick like Chemise is a lot of work and if you have a little dick, it's even more work. What man can take all that pressure?

I guess that's why Chemise wants a nigga like me. That's why white men will call on a nigga like me. When they can't take the pressure, I'm the pressure cooker. I can put in some real serious work.

Chemise interrupts my thoughts with her words.

"Let me turn on my back, baby. Let's get back in the missionary position."

I remember she said that's how she likes it to be when she comes so I quickly flip her ass over. Then I start going for broke and ramming my dick deeply inside of her.

"Oh, yes, Mandingo! Fuck me! I love you, daddy. Fuck me with this dick. Please, fuck. Please, fuck me."

As her words trail off she grabs me really tightly and starts having spasms underneath me. I've taken her to ecstasy and she's loving it.

When she finally regains her composure, she seems intent on making me come.

"Oh, hell no," she says. "You're not walking away from this good pussy without coming."

She still thinks her pussy is so damn good.

She wiggles from underneath of me and pushes me down on my back. Then she starts sucking my dick almost as good as Karen Steinberg did. The slurping sounds indicate how possessed she is to make me nut. I'm just happy to be getting my dick sucked.

I start to realize why she likes the mirrors. I didn't notice until now that a real faint strobe light is directed toward the ceiling. The effect is really erotic.

Her nice plump ass is staring down at me from the mirror and it's having an effect on me I didn't expect. The whole scene is a turn on. That, coupled with the surgery her mouth is performing on my dick, ultimately becomes too much for me. I feel myself tensing up.

"Yes, Chemise. Suck on that big black dick. Suck on it!"

Her mouth is too much for me and before I know it, I'm shooting.

Like Karen Steinberg, Chemise swallows every drop. I'm totally turned on by the black woman living inside the white woman's life. Her body is the truth just like a black woman's and her mannerisms are freaky just like a white woman's. I'm not mad at Chemise at all. She gets a thumbs up.

When she leaves me to freshen up, I realize how tired I am.

The bitch really put me to some serious work. All I want to do is take a nap.

I find out quickly, though, that there won't be any sleeping here. Chemise comes out of the bathroom and lets me know right away what time it is.

"Mandingo, you are priceless. I have to admit that I was skeptical when Denise told me about you. But she didn't lie at all. Not many men can hang with me like you did. You held your own beautifully. So much so that I don't want you to leave. But hubby will be home in an hour and you know what that means. I've fallen in love for love before but that's a terrible place to be. Your dick is the bomb but you can't give me what he gives me."

"What do you mean, Chemise? I'm not trying to hold you down. I thought this was just business."

"Exactly. And business is business. You fucked the shit out of me and I loved it but our little roll in the hay is over."

I still looked at her dumfounded. That prompted her to say what she had to say in plain English.

"Mandingo, I love you and everything. But like they say in the clubs, you ain't got to go home but you got to get the hell out of here. My husband's about to come home."

"Oh shit! My bad. Why didn't you just say so?"

I jumped up and start getting dressed.

"I really do wish you could stay, Mandingo. I haven't felt this good in a long time."

"That's fine. I'm kind of tired so I need to be going."

"Please don't be mad at me. You know my situation."

"I'm not mad. You ain't my wifey or nothing like that."

"You are mad. I'm sorry baby. I did mean it when I told you that I loved you."

I look at her like, "Yeah right."

"I mean it. It was love at first sight. And after you did to me what you did, umm. No one has ever made me feel that good."

"I know, right. But I still have to go."

"Please, baby don't pout."

Chemise was gone and the rich white bitch Mrs. Goutier had returned.

"Mommy will take care of you real good."

"My mom is dead, OK?"

"Please, baby, don't be like that."

She opens one of the bedroom's three walk-in closets and comes out with a handful of cash.

"I've already paid Denise. She has your money. I don't know what kind of a split you get so I won't mention the amount. That's between you and her. Still, take this as a tip."

I take the money from her and notice that there are no twenties or tens in the stack. And it's a really large stack.

"This is a lot of fucking money, Chemise."

"It's ten thousand and you deserve every cent of it. Don't tell Denise, OK? Keep it all for yourself. She's already been paid, remember? And next time I would really like to call you directly."

"I appreciate all of that but you're going to have to go through Denise next time, too. She's done a lot for me and I'm loyal to her. I don't ever want her to doubt that."

"I just hope that you're still single if I ever decide to divorce my husband. I'm sure I'll walk away with a good piece of change."

"I'll keep that in mind, Chemise. But right now, I have to go."

She looks at her watch.

"Wait, Mandingo. We have over forty minutes."

"What does that mean?"

"I did give you a good tip, baby. Can you humor me for a minute?"

"OK. You're right. What's up?"

She doesn't answer me. She just grabs my hand and leads me down the staircase.

She takes me into a room that I didn't see on the tour.

"My husband doesn't know that I know but he fucked some bitch in this room before. How can he do that when he doesn't even have the strength to satisfy me, his wife?"

"Why are you telling me this?"

Again, she doesn't answer me. She pushes me against the wall and pulls down my zipper.

This time when she starts sucking my dick she does some shit that Karen Steinberg couldn't even understand. If it were a word, Karen Steinberg couldn't even pronounce it.

In less than three minutes, I'm shooting my come into her mouth. And again, she swallows every drop.

"I just needed to know that I wasn't loosing it, Mandingo. That's all. I won't hold you up any longer. I know you have to go."

This is some crazy shit. I just fucked the hell out of a dimepiece and walked away with ten thousand dollars in my pocket. And I got to come in her mouth not once but twice.

I can get used to this.

I can really get used to this.

CHAPTER NINE

Denise

I'm anxious to see what Mandingo says about Mrs. Goutier when he comes to collect his fifteen hundred dollars.

Mrs. Goutier is far from ugly. He should feel like I just hooked his ass up. I know Mandingo is a titty man and Mrs. Goutier has some nice fucking titties. I used to love sucking on them. Too bad she got out of her lesbian phase. She was one of my best tipping customers.

Mrs. Goutier's pussy was much bigger and more ran through than mine. She's obviously had a lot of dicks in her life. But that didn't prevent it from tasting sweet as hell. As a matter of fact, I used to affectionately call her Succulent because she smelled fruity and exotic. It always seemed like her body had a splash of cream.

I used to like licking her pussy from the back. I loved the way her ass poked in the air when I stuck my tongue inside her.

And I loved the way she would talk nasty to me. That was

such a fucking turn on.

She wasn't from the hood but there was something about taking her body to the Land of Orgasms that made her want to curse and talk mad shit.

"Lick this fucking pussy, you black bitch. Eat it, you whore. Eat my fucking pussy."

Mrs. Goutier was crazy. But her mouthpiece urged me on more than enough times. While I was eating her pussy, my shit got wetter than hers. It was flowing like a faucet. And when it overflowed, Mrs. Goutier never hesitated to help soak up the spill.

"Lay down you black bitch and let me sop up those pussy juices."

She instructed me like a drill sergeant and I made every attempt to be her best recruit. I never hesitated. I always gave her exactly what she asked for as quickly was humanly possible.

"OK, Mrs. Goutier." I always maintained my professionalism when I addressed her. "Is this how you want me?"

Rarely did she answer me. She just slid her head down between my legs and started going to town. I felt like I was vacationing in Sin City because something that felt so good had to be a sin.

Thoughts of Ms. Goutier are making me horny as hell. I look out the window one more time for Mandingo before laying back on the couch and pulling up my nightie. I just have to touch myself and fantasize about her. I have to have Mrs. Goutier take care of me once again.

Yet no sooner than I place my finger inside myself do I

hear a car pull up outside. Seconds later, Mandingo is knocking at the door. I am so frustrated that he messed up my groove.

"Wait, nigga, I'm coming."

I open up the door to his smiling face. I can tell from his expression that Ms. Goutier has his ass running on half a tank.

"Hey, Mandingo. You look tired. Come lay down. You look like you could use a nap. I'll get you your money."

"Nah, I'm cool. I wasn't gonna stay. I need to take care of something."

"Nigga, what the hell do you have to do?" I'm starting to get pissed and I don't even know why. "You don't have any classes right now."

"I'm just tired, that's all. I just want to…"

"Wait." I cut him off. "Did you not hear me tell you that you can lay down here and take a nap? What, now that you fucked me a couple of times you don't want to chill with me anymore?"

I want to take the words back as soon as I say them. But I know I can't. So I just go with the flow and decide to play it by ear.

"You know that's not true, Denise. You're the only person around here who has any love for me. And you know I love you. You're the one who doesn't want to take the next step."

I'm glad I waited for him to come out of his face.

"I do have love for you, Mandingo, but you should fall back on the love thing. Let's just enjoy our friendship and take things one day at a time. Yes, we'll fuck now and again. Hell, I may even cook for you from time to time. But, you just can't sprint out of the blocks like you're Carl Lewis. Let's handle our business and do this the right way. And above everything else, let's not ruin our friendship. Now, because I care about you, will you please just do what I say and come lay down? You look tired as hell."

"OK. But if you plan on touching me, I should go take a shower first. I never got a chance to at Mrs. Goutier's."

I immediately get chills.

"Nah, you're fine just the way you are."

Now I'm planning on sucking his dick just to taste her juices. I need some resolution to the shit that's been on my mind for the past hour.

"Just lay down next to me and I'll take care of you."

I strip him down to his boxers and take off my nightie. I get in the bed with him, wearing only a thong. Then I proceed to give his dick surgery with my mouth, licking up every hint of Mrs. Goutier.

After a while, I get on top and ride the shit out of his dick. When he nuts inside of me, I shiver and splash out gallons of my own juices all over him. Then I fall asleep with his dick still inside of me.

A part of me feels like I never want to wake up, that this is how it should be forever, without a worry in the world.

CHAPTER TEN

Mandingo

I wake up with Denise laying on top of me, her wet pussy tightly wrapped around my dick. She must have had her way with me after I gave up arguing with her and fell asleep.

I wanted some definition to what we were doing. All Denise wanted to do was fuck the shit out of each other. Finally, I told her I would not be used and manipulated and collapsed. I guess she got her way after all.

I have to admit, though, that it's a big ego boost to have someone as fly as Denise want my dick so badly she just takes it from me without my permission. If I had a pussy between my legs, I think it would have been called rape.

But it wasn't. All it was was a man fulfilling his tribal duty to give the woman his dick. And judging by how wet her pussy is, the damned thing did right proper.

*****

Not only is the thought of Denise needing my dick so bad stroking my ego, it's also making me horny as hell. And the fact that her pussy is already wrapped around my dick gives me more than convenient access to her. In an instant, my thoughts make me hard as a rock.

Even though Denise is asleep, the awakening of my sleeping giant makes her moan. I decide to be sneaky and try to fuck her without waking her up.

Maybe she'll say something insightful in her sleep.

I arch my back and grab her waist and begin to slowly and carefully move my dick in and out of her tight pussy. Immediately, her breathing becomes broken by long sighs and moans. Yet she remains fast asleep.

I pick up the speed a little but not too fast. I don't want her to wake up. Something tells me that I'm going to find what I'm searching for.

As her pussy starts pulsating and I feel her juices start to gush out, I hear something that's music to my ears.

"Yes, baby, fuck me. I need you so bad. Fuck me like I know you know how."

I smile widely. She has to be talking about me.

"Give it to me, baby. Oooh, give it to me baby..."

She opens her eyes. "Mandingo, what are you doing up?"

"I think the question is what are you doing while you're sleeping?"

"I wasn't doing shit but trying to get some sleep."

"I guess that explains why your wet pussy is all wrapped around this dick."

"I don't know what you're talking about. If you weren't my boy I would scream rape. Now, can you please take your dick out of me?"

"You're the one who put it in there in the first place so you're the one who's gonna have to take it out."

"You're such a smart ass. If you weren't so damned cocky maybe I would give your ass some more often."

She gets off of me and climbs out the bed.

I ponder her words and try to figure out how to come back. I know what time it is and she knows what time it is as far as her stealing some dick. But I'm not sure what I'm gonna gain by continuing to pull her card. I decide to get up and stand behind her. I start rubbing her arms while she's looking through the blinds out the window.

"Look, Denise. The truth is, you're fabulous. And I don't know what I would've done without you after my family died. But you have my head spinning. I don't know which way is up. I guess the only way I can hear that you dig me is to find a way to say the words myself. You never have and I doubt you ever will."

"Mandingo, you're alright. What else do you want me to say?"

"Something! Anything! Hell, let me know what you're feeling."

"Right now, my pussy is feeling a little sore. Is that good enough for you?"

I vigorously resist the urge to show her how proud I'm feeling right now. I decide to be as supportive as someone who is clueless as can be.

"I'm sorry, I think. I don't know what happened. I was sound asleep."

"I know you were sleeping, Mandingo. But you need to

get your ego in check. You don't even know the whole story."

"It seems pretty obvious to me." I backslide. "Is there another way to take waking up and finding you straddling me with a dripping sex box?"

"OK. Now I'm pissed. I was trying to spare your feelings but since you're being a smart ass."

"Spare me?"

"Yes, spare you."

"Spare me how, Denise?" I ask her sarcastically while poking my chest out. I know that in less than ten seconds she was gonna have to admit that I am the man.

"OK, Mandingo. Since you asked, I'll fill you in. I was jealous that Mrs. Goutier wanted to be with you and not me. Initially, it had me fuming. But eventually I started thinking back to the times she and I had together. And I had just started masturbating on the couch thinking about her when I heard you pull up. So, while you were thinking I was lusting over you when I invited you to bed, I was just thinking about sucking Mrs. Goutier's juices off your dick. So, are you happy now?"

I ponder her question for a while.

"No. I'm not really happy. Not yet."

Denise looks at me sideways so I continue.

"What does tasting her pussy juices have to do with jumping on this dick and riding it?"

"Duh? You had the bitch that I used to be in love with earlier. So I had to have you so I could feel like she wasn't getting one up on me. This doesn't have a damned thing to do with you. This is woman shit that you couldn't possibly understand."

"Whatever." I don't understand and don't even feel like trying. "Can we finish fucking now?"

"Did you miss the part where I said my pussy was sore? You are such a fucking dunce!"

"Well, can you just give me my money so I can bounce? I'm tired of the abuse I'm getting around here."

"You're gonna ask me for money after everything we've been through? I know Mrs. Goutier tipped the shit out of you."

"If I remember correctly, after you fucked the shit out of me you told me that it was just business. So it's nothing personal, Denise. It's just business."

"I got your money, nigga. But you're gonna have to start paying my ass back since you felt the need to ask for it."

"Now you're throwing shit up in my face."

"Like you didn't start it."

"I'm leaving. What was I supposed to do?"

"Wait for me to mention it and give it to you just like I've been waiting for you to mention it and grease my palms. The shit works both ways."

"Keep the fucking money, Denise, if it's like that."

I start stomping around, gathering my things so I can get dressed and get away from her as quickly as possible.

"I don't give a shit about you pouting, Mandingo. You're the one who threw your fifteen hundred dollars up in my face. I'm just reminding you who I am and who you are."

"Who the fuck am I, Denise?"

She gets all up in my face.

"The same motherfucker I've been caring for since you got here. Or did you forget about that shit?"

I step down off the ledge.

"OK, Denise. You're right. I apologize. You have been there for me and I was wrong to do you like that. But I still don't want the money."

"You just don't get it! It's not about the money. I can give you the money. Why would I need your punk-ass fifteen hundred dollars anyway with all the money I have?"

"The thought had crossed my mind."

Denise rolls her eyes before continuing to reprimand me.

"It's the principle, Mandingo. Aside from an occasional joke or two, when have I ever come at you about money? When have I ever tried to make you feel like you were taking advantage of me?"

"I can't say that you have, Denise, but now you have me fucking people to earn a dollar. You know how I feel about it. How many times have I told you that you should do something else with your brains?"

"And how many times did you worry about how many dicks and clits I sucked when you were grabbing food out of my refrigerator?"

"That's not fair, Denise."

"How come it's not fair? It's the truth. I've been doing what I have to do without comments from the peanut gallery. All niggas do is talk shit about what I do for a living while they're washing their dicks so they can go home to their wives. Or in your case, while they're living lovely off the kindness of my heart."

I start feeling some type of way. "You're getting real personal, Denise ."

"It's about time I did, too. You always have so much to say

about what I do but you never turn down my tainted money. If it was such a problem for you, you would have preferred to starve than take a thing from me. Short of that, you're a fucking hypocrite who won't pull me out of the ocean. You just keep reminding me that I'm about to drown if I don't get out. Well, if you ain't gonna be a part of the solution, don't even fucking mention the problem."

She was right, but I couldn't tell her that.

"It seems like I struck a nerve with you, and I don't see anything productive coming out of us throwing bombs at each other. I still love you and I hope this discussion doesn't mess up our friendship."

"I love you too, Mandingo, but I'm tired of you coming at my neck. I'm handling my business, that's all. And I suggest you do the same instead of acting all holier than thou."

"You're right. But I still have to be out. I have to take care of a couple of things."

I kiss her on the cheek and she kisses me softly and tenderly on the mouth.

"Just enjoy the ride, man, and stop being so uptight. There're a lot of other men out there who would love to be in your shoes right now."

*****

I know Denise's last words are totally on point.

I craved her from the moment I met her. And now that I've been with her a few times and have the opportunity to keep being with her, I'm trying to find ways to screw it up. I need to seriously check myself and fall back off of my petty bullshit. Like she said, I need to stop being so uptight.

CHAPTER ELEVEN

Mandingo

Eating really good food calms and relaxes me. So I decide to check out one of my aunts today. But I have some business to take care of first.

I track down a gypsy cab and ask the driver to take me to 125th Street. I want to open up an account at Commerce Bank.

He tells me that it's gonna be eight dollars for the ride so I ask him how much he'd charge to drive me around for an hour.

"That will be a hundred bucks, my man."

"Alright. But I need you to be where I need you to be. Don't get messed up with the cops and get chased away."

"OK. But you have to give me half now."

I look at him sideways.

"I'm not trying to cheat you, my man. I work for a living and have no problem with earning my money. I want no parts of the wrath of Jah."

"I feel you. But you'll get your eight bucks when we get to the bank and a hundred if you're still there after I come out. I already told you I don't have time to be playing with the cops today."

"I guess that's up to you, my man."

*****

I decide to deposit seven hundred dollars in the bank. My plan is to keep putting money in the bank a little at a time so nothing looks suspicious.

After opening an account, I have the cabbie take me to Queens so I can pick up an inconspicuous ride.

Three thousand dollars later, I drive off the lot with a 1999 Honda Accord. It's clean and drives like a champion but won't catch the attention of New York City's so-called finest.

*****

Since I'm in Queens, and since my stomach is growling like crazy, I decide to check out Aunt Kadija. I'm hoping she has something nice brewing on the stove.

*****

As soon as I walk in the door, I'm reminded why it's been such a long while since I've visited her. After hugs, and then kisses on my cheeks, she immediately starts talking.

She must have forgotten that she already told me what she's telling me again — about Uncle Moriba and how lonely she feels all the time. I didn't want to hear it then and I certainly don't want to sit through it again.

So as she's beating up on my ears, I look around the brownstone and realize that if I wasn't sure I came in through the same old front door I always come in through, I'd think I was in the wrong house.

The floors look different and I realize that's because they're brand spanking new hardwood that's so shiny I can see my reflection. The raggedy old living room set is gone and in its place is a plush leather set draped with furry throws that look like real animal skin. The cocktail and end tables are dark solid oak and shiny brass. And sitting on top of them are matching antique lamps that look like they came from some rich white person's charity auction.

Goddamn. Uncle Moriba must have won the lottery.

"Aunt Kadija, I don't know why you're so upset. Obviously Uncle Moriba is working really hard to make a nice home for you."

"Yes, but I'm all by myself. What good is this shit if I don't have anyone to share it with? And I'm the damned fool. I'm more mad at myself than him. I don't have to be alone and lonely."

I take in Aunt Kadija's loveliness. She's right. She doesn't have to wait on my uncle. She's too gorgeous to even be with him in the first place.

Her silky robe is draped loosely over her body and I see that her outrage is getting to her because her nipples are pushing through the fabric.

I'm not sure why Uncle Moriba leaves her home all alone without even checking on her. She's some kind of hot. But then, almost as if on cue, she starts talking again.

Her nostrils start flaring so now I know she's angry. But her expression doesn't make her look ugly. It makes her look even more sexy. She reminds me of a hot-blooded latina, so full of fire that it turns you the fuck on. For a minute I had to fall back and remind myself that she's my aunt.

"What fucking man can leave all this?" she hollers after jumping up off the couch and opening up her robe, revealing two of the most beautiful titties I've ever seen. And to be truthful, her bald pussy looks pretty good, too.

"Aunt Kadija, close your robe, please. Uncle Moriba would freak out if he walked in here right now."

"Fuck him! And I don't understand you either. Do you like men or something? Why would you complain about looking at all of this? I'd think you'd be trying to touch me."

"Actually, Aunt Kadija, I love the shit out of women. And if it weren't inappropriate, I would be trying to rub all over you right now. But..."

"That sounds good, Mandingo," she interrupts. "It would be nice for someone to be touching me right about now." She starts rubbing herself in all the right places.

"Aunt Kadija, stop!" I jump up and try to close her robe. Maybe I should have stayed sitting down.

She grabs me and pulls herself into me. Her body feels so warm against mine. My manhood reacts immediately.

"See, Mandingo. You know what you're standing next to and you're happy to be doing it. Why can't your uncle understand what he has?"

"Can you let me go, please, Aunt Kadija? This is not right and it looks beyond suspicious."

"This doesn't look suspicious, Mandingo. This looks suspicious." She starts rubbing my dick through my jeans. I become even more aroused.

"Aunt Kadija, what are you doing?"

"Do you want me to stop?"

"Yes. No. I don't know. This is not right."

"What your uncle is doing to me isn't right."

"So you plan to use me for revenge?"

"Not revenge, Mandingo. I've been wanting to take a bite out of your sexy ass since I met you. So, since your Uncle Moriba is doing for him, I may as well do for me. Why should he be the only one who's having his cake and eating it too?"

"I can't fuck my uncle's wife."

"You don't have to. I'll fuck you."

Before I know what's happening, my zipper is down and Aunt Kadija is sucking my dick like she's trying to make my fifteen inches turn into twenty. It's some kind of special.

As she's slurping, she unlatches my belt and unbuttons my pants, pulling them down until they are bunched up near my ankles.

Next, I feel her untying my shoelaces. Like a zombie, I lift my feet one at a time so she can take my pants off.

Before long, her French-manicured fingers are unbuttoning my button down shirt and scraping against my chest. Before I know it, my shirt is on the floor beside my pants and shoes.

My ecstasy is so intense, I barely notice that Aunt Kadija has stood up and removed her robe.

I'm in a daze. My aunt is bent at the waist in front of me, sucking and slurping for dear life, and I've got her butter-soft ass in my hands. Where has she been hiding it all these years? It's not outrageous like Aunt Mariam's but I'd give it a ten on my score card anyway. It's up there.

In fact, Aunt Kadija's total package is up there. She could have any man strung the fuck out. So why in the world she's playing around with my uncle, I don't know.

I feel myself falling backwards and come out of my trance enough to realize that Aunt Kadija's pushing me down on the couch.

Before I can utter a word in protest, she's climbing on top of me. She forces my big dick inside her tight little pussy then lets out a grunt. Its length and width catches her by surprise just as it does with every woman. That first thrust into their pussies always makes them gasp.

I feel her getting wetter almost immediately.

Goddamn! Wet and tight! She's killing me.

I'm already thinking about how I'm never going to find the strength to do the right thing. Her pussy's too damned good.

Aunt Kadija. We are never doing this again. I can't start having an affair with my aunt.

As soon as I think the words, she starts writhing on top of me and riding me like she's a Texas cowgirl. It's almost like she can hear me thinking and her body is answering, "Oh yes, the fuck you can!"

Her pussy is so wet and tight and her movements are so skilled, she doesn't get to do the love dance for long. Three minutes and I pop.

When she feels my dick jerking, she jumps up off me.

"No, Mandingo!"

In an instant, her lips are wrapped around my dick and she's sucking up every ounce of me that didn't already find it's way inside her luscious pussy.

My mouth is screaming but no sounds come out. She's taken me to a place where not even Denise has taken me. The thrill of it all has me overwhelmed.

*****

I feel so turned on that I'm hot and burning. The walls are pressing against my head. Everything is moving in circles a mile a minute. Aunt Kadija's fucked me in some type of way. I'm seriously tripping. I've never known ecstasy like this before.

Uncle Moriba gets mad props from me. How the fuck can he leave this pussy sitting here, alone?

Before I know it, I'm so turned on that I feel myself drifting off. But I'm not sleeping. I'm fainting.

*****

"Mandingo. Mandingo!"

I hear someone calling my name but the voice seems far away. Eventually, though, it gets closer. And, finally, it sounds familiar.

When I open my eyes, I see Aunt Kadija's beautiful face. She's wiping my forehead with a cold, damp cloth.

"I've done some damage in my time but I can't say I've ever made anyone pass out," she says, smiling.

"I think it's because I'm so hungry. I haven't eaten all

94

day."

"Well, I made some stewed chicken. I'll fix you a bowl."

I start rustling like I'm about to get up but she gently nudges me back down.

"Don't be silly. Lay right there. I'll get it for you," she says with a twinkle in her eye. "Now don't you be thinking that you're gonna come around here to fuck your Aunt Kadija and get food whenever you feel like it."

A couple of minutes later, she's sitting in front of me feeding me stewed chicken like I'm the king of the fucking earth. I eat every bit.

Aunt Kadija gets up to take my plate to the kitchen and I watch her ass jiggle as she walks away. Her strut is fierce and confident, her body is divine, and her entire presentation is unprecedented. I start to wonder if Uncle Moriba is blackmailing her.

Maybe he helped her get her citizenship or something. Someone like her should not be with an asshole like him.

Aunt Kadija returns with a pillow and a blanket. "Lay down here and rest yourself, child, until you get all your strength back."

"Don't you think I should put my clothes on first?"

"No. I'll just fold them up. You're in my house and I want you to be comfortable. Besides, I might get the urge to sneak back down here a little later if you feel like you're up to it. You didn't even give me five minutes."

She smiles at me and walks away. I don't even have the energy to laugh. I close my eyes and immediately drift off to sleep.

*****

I wake up with Aunt Kadija writhing on top of me. She feels just as good this time as she did the last time.

"Aunt Kadija, you feel so good but this is so wrong," I tell her. I'm praying she won't stop but I know that she has to.

"Don't call me Auntie," she says. "You make it sound so wrong when it feels so right. Call me baby or something... anything."

I can't stop myself. "Yes, baby," I swoon. "Baby, yes."

"Oh, Mandingo, this is heaven."

Aunt Kadija rides me with the expertise of a bull rider. Her hips hug my thighs and her thighs are pressing against me for dear life. There's no way she's going to fall off until she takes me and herself to the place we went to not long ago. I have no idea what time it is and I don't care. I'm just glad that she woke me up to such a treat. The woman is a goddess. Uncle Moriba is the biggest fucking fool in the world.

****

After we come together, again, Aunt Kadija throws her arms around my neck and hugs me like she'll never let me go. I like how she feels in my arms and don't want to let her go but she breaks free.

"Wait," I say. "Please don't go. Can I talk to you for a while?"

"Of course," she says. "What's on your mind?"

"I have to be honest with you," I start. "This whole thing is freaking me out. Don't get it twisted. You are not freaking me out. The fact that Uncle Moriba is not here with you is freaking me out. How can he have all this and not spend more time with you?"

"That's the exact argument we had just last night, Mandingo," she admits. "In fact, we have that argument all the time. But you need to understand that I'm not the exception to the rule. Many other women are going through the same exact thing I'm going through."

"But they can't be as good as you," I say. "They can't be half as good as you."

"Shit," she says, laughing. "I appreciate the compliment but not only are some of them as good as me, some are even a lot better. It has nothing to do with us. It has everything to do with our men."

"But why?" I ask. "You could leave. You shouldn't allow yourself to be subjected to Uncle Moriba's bullshit."

"Leave and go where, Mandingo?" she asks. "Don't you think the next man will treat me the same way? He'd be nice and sweet in the beginning but as soon as he feels comfortable, he'll start giving me bullshit just like your uncle does. And how would I know if his bullshit will be worse than your uncle's? A woman never knows. She just hopes and prays. I swear women have been hoping and praying about no-good-ass men for as far back as history can take us. Men fuck up, Mandingo. That's what you do. The chase is more important to men than the day to day reality after the capture. Maybe you wouldn't be as bad to me as your uncle is because you recognize that I'm special, but you wouldn't be perfect either."

"I couldn't be perfect," I say, defending myself. "You're

married to my uncle."

"Don't be snide, Mandingo. If by chance we met in a gro-cery store and you stepped to me and I was with it, you'd be a knight in shining armor for a while. But once you got what you wanted, day by day your armor would rust. And eventu-ally, I would no longer see the promise in you that I see right now."

"That's not fair," I say. "Who's to say I wouldn't do right by you? But anyway, we would never get together because if I saw you in a grocery store, I wouldn't talk to you."

"Why not?" she asks.

"Because I'm a broke-ass student. What would make me think that I'd have a chance with a woman like you?"

"That's where you're wrong, Mandingo," she says. "That's where all men are wrong. You think that all a woman wants from a man is money. That's why you go out there in the world to get her all kinds of stuff. You buy furniture here and jewelry there but never take the time to connect with a woman on an emotional level. You just get her more stuff. And the one thing she needs, she never gets. Your undivided attention and your uncompromising love. A woman needs to feel special to her man. She needs to know that she matters. It was no coincidence that I started wearing robes whenever you came over. I've seen how you look at me, and I've been dying for that attention. When I stopped getting it from Mori-ba, I started wanting to get it from anywhere. I'm not saying that you're just anybody, but if Moriba was doing rigth by me, none of this would ever have happened. In a nutshell, most women cheat because their men take them for granted. Like they say, idle time is the devil's workplace. If you leave your woman alone too often, waiting and wanting, what do you expect? Devotion? If a man isn't taking care of his woman, you can best believe that the woman will look for a man who will. While you are out there partying, bullshitting and acting like you are the rulers of the fucking world, your women are home, miserable. We yearn for the companionship we aren't getting from you. And eventually, we'll find it elsewhere. And what's even more fucked up is that your Uncle Moriba would never in a million years think it would happen. He thinks that what little he gives me is enough. All men think they give a lot. But eventually, they find out that it's not a lot and it's not enough. And what's worse is that when they do find out, they don't take any responsibility. They blame it on the woman or the other man. And all they had to do in the first place was pay attention to their queen. So, to answer your question—I've been babbling—there is nothing wrong with me. Where does the bullshit come from that's implanted in a little boy's mind? Not his mother. There's something wrong with society. And women get all the blame when we finally say enough is enough. It's all the man's fault. He'll lose the best thing he ever had because his brain is stuck on stupid. Your Uncle Moriba, he thinks he's punishing me by staying away after our last argument. But he's the one who's being punished. This pussy used to be his. Now it's yours, if you want it. And if you do, hopefully you've taken heed to this conversation. I've shown you the best of the best, and I've just gotten started. I'm nowhere near done. So let's see if you are able take care of me and treat my heart better than he did."

After she finishes her speech, Aunt Kadija plants a steaming kiss on my mouth and turns to walk back upstairs. Yet the twinkle in her eye tells me that she may be back for another round. And I'm actually looking forward to it.

"Damn, Uncle Moriba! Your dumb-ass doesn't know what it's missing," I say as I close my eyes and eventually drift off to sleep.

CHAPTER TWELVE

Moriba

It's Friday night and ordinarily I would be with Kadija but she pissed me off last night.

I called Fateema up instead and bribed her into chilling with me by taking her to Saks Fifth Avenue and letting her pick out a few outfits.

*****

I love Kadija more than my other wives. But sometimes you have to put your foot down.

I have to let her know that I make the rules and she does as I say. I can't let her keep sweating me for time. I'm a busy man and busy men do what busy men do.

What she's gonna do is just sit her ass in that plush house and be happy.

How can she be lonely in a house like that anyway? Some

people would kill to be surrounded by so much luxury.

That's the problem with women. And that's why her ass is home and I'm out spending money on Fateema. Then I'm gonna fuck the shit out of her.

Kadija needs to learn that if she keeps her mouth shut, she won't be punished. I'm the man of the house and she does what I say. Staying home with no hope of getting some dick until Sunday morning is what the fuck she gets. Maybe next time she'll remember who's holding all the cards. I'm the head nigga in motherfucking charge.

*****

Fateema calls out to me.

"Moriba, tell me how my outfit looks."

Without saying a word, I get up and go just outside the dressing room.

She comes out in a pair of tight fitting, Versace bell-bottoms. She's hooked it up with a rosy-colored linen shirt that matches perfectly with one of the prominent colors in the pants.

Her ass looks unbelievable in the pants. It's poking out like a little girl's pout when she can't have her way.

Her stomach looks as nonexistent as ever. I want to lick the Moriba tattoo that surrounds her belly so that I can kiss myself while I'm kissing her.

I remember the days when she was so hot for me she got the tattoo. She's still big on me now but backed off because I backed off her when she said she didn't want any kids. But with the way she's looking right now, I want to be all up in her space.

She has the bottom of the shirt tied in a knot to accentuate her lovely and vivacious breasts. I feel like mushing my face between her cleavage right now. I'm totally turned on.

"Moriba! Tell me what you think."

Her voice interrupts my thoughts.

"I think you look so damned good that I could take you right in the dressing room right now."

She smiles.

"Now that's something we've never done, baby. So you do like what I have on? You know I want to please you."

"I love what you have on. And you can please me. You can please me right now."

I motion towards the dressing room with my eyes and she smiles seductively.

Fateema seems to be on the same page as I am. She sensually backs into the dressing room, her eyes telling me to follow.

We close and lock the door and I immediately start to undress her. We kiss passionately as every shred of her soon to be purchased clothing comes off.

I don't have time to get undressed so I just pull my pants down around my ankles.

Before I get a chance to turn her around and put myself inside her, Fateema drops in front of me and starts kissing my dick. She kisses and sucks and takes me back to our old days.

"It's been so long since you've sucked it like this, baby."

"It's been so long since you've asked to be with me on a Friday night."

"I thought you didn't want to."

"Yeah, I said that. But you didn't have to agree so fast. You showed me how important I am. You didn't put up the least bit of a fight. Anyway, stop interrupting me so I can concentrate on sucking this dick."

I happily oblige her.

When she's ready for me, she sits me down on the little bench and finds a way to straddle me. Then she proceeds to fuck the shit out of me, just as she did in happier times.

"Don't you miss this pussy, Moriba? Don't you want it more often?"

"Yes, baby, yes. I do want it more often. I do."

Fateema smiles and fucks me like she's possessed.

At this point, I'm in the realm of utter and complete ecstasy. I'll agree to anything she asks of me. I don't care. I just want to feel like this as often as I'm able.

"Nobody can do me like this, baby. Nobody can," I tell her.

Fateema smiles at my comments and continues to put it on me. I feel like I'm the male version of Stella and I'm getting my groove back.

*****

Just as I feel myself about to come, I hear a knock on the door.

"You've been in there too long," says an authoritative voice. "You need to be wrapping it up so other people can get in there."

"I'll just be a minute," Fateema says, winded.

"I do have a key, ma'am."

"And I have a lawyer. Get the fuck out of here!"

I guess he relents because I don't hear him anymore.

"We do have to hurry up, Fateema."

"I know but it feels so good."

"It does feel good. It feels damned good."

She grinds herself into me and the voice of authority quickly leaves my head. I get back to the place where I was before I heard him speak, which was just a few pumps away from having a screaming orgasm.

"Oh shit, Fateema! Oh shit."

I nut inside her hard and long. I feel like at least a pint of semen leaves me and enters her.

"We have to have a part two in Harlem," she says.

"I'm game if you're game."

I immediately think about what type of excuse I'm going to come up with for Kadija.

I put a caring and loving look back on my face and kiss her passionately on the mouth. My tongue dances with hers and it feels like we're the same lovers we were when we were hot and heavy.

"Should we start getting dressed, Fateema, before Rambo comes back?"

"Yeah. We have all night to finish this."

Damn. My story is gonna have to be better than I thought.

CHAPTER THIRTEEN

Mandingo

I feel a nudge and see Aunt Kadija standing over me with her robe on.

"It's one thirty in the morning, Mandingo. You may as well come up to bed. If your uncle hasn't come by now, he's not coming."

"What makes you so sure? I don't want any drama to pop off."

"I'm positive, Mandingo. I wouldn't put you in the middle of our bullshit. Just come to bed. You need to stretch out."

I collect my clothes and follow Aunt Kadija up the stairs. Right now, I definitely don't want any drama. I just want a good night's sleep.

Aunt Kadija takes off her robe and we get into bed and cuddle up, butt naked. But there's no more sex. We fall asleep hugging each other. I feel like this has been one of the most special days of my life.

*****

Early Saturday morning I get a call on the cell phone Denise bought me. I know it's her since she's the only one who has the number.

"We have to talk," she says without even saying hello.

"What's wrong?"

"Just get here as fast as you can."

With that, she's gone.

"Is everything OK?" Aunt Kadija asks me.

"Yeah. I have to go, that's all. I'm kind of new at this job."

"Well, I didn't mean to make you oversleep. You should have told me. And I wanted to fix you some breakfast before you left."

"That's OK, Auntie. It's not your fault. I'm always on call and never know when they're gonna give me some hours. I should have time to eat, though. They don't know I have a car. They probably think I'm taking the subway."

Without a word, Aunt Kadija pops up and leans down to put on her robe. In the early morning light, her body is even more spectacular. Her sex is the bomb, and man, can she cook!

Minutes after she disappears, I smell wonderful things permeating the air. I also hear Bob Marley blasting on the radio.

"I don't wanna wait in vain for your love..."

I'm not sure if she's telling me something or in defiance to my uncle. I still can't understand why he's not trying to be with her twenty-four seven.

I guess some men just need to be players. Now me, on the other hand, if a woman is making me happy, there's no need for me to go astray. I'll stick with her and do what I have to to make things work.

*****

Aunt Kadija comes upstairs with a plate of scrambled eggs with cheese, turkey breakfast sausages, home fries, grits, croissants with butter, and fresh squeezed orange juice.

Just like last night, she starts to feed me and it looks as if she plans to feed me every drop.

As I'm luxuriating in her attention and feeling important, my cell phone goes off. Of course, it's Denise.

"What's up, Denise?"

"Where are you? You've been out all night?"

"Stop playing, Denise. Do you need something? If not, I'll call you later. I'm kind of busy right now."

"Busy? Busy? Nigga, you're tryna say you're too busy for me?"

"If you're gonna be joking and stuff, yeah. Just tell me what's up."

"What's up is I need to talk to you about something face to face. So get your ass here as soon as possible. And not take your time as soon as possible. I mean ASAP, as soon as possible."

Click.

*****

As I drive the last few blocks before I get to Denise, I'm wondering what the fuck is on her mind.

If I had taken her seriously, I would have missed out on a

dick sucking that was even better than last night's, if that's even possible.

Aunt Kadija put so much of my dick in her mouth and sucked the shit so hard I thought I was gonna faint. I wonder again what the hell is up with my uncle.

*****

Denise opens the door before I even get a chance to knock.

"So you're laughing at me now?"

"Denise, what the fuck are you talking about?" I look at her sideways yet she doesn't budge from her stance or appear as if she's going to back down. I try to ease up a little even though I'm confused. "For real, Denise, what's wrong with you? I must be missing something."

Denise

Every part of me is saying to just back off and start laughing. I should play the whole thing off like it's a joke. But I can't. I've been initiated into the league of Mandingo and it seems like I'm losing my power to remain calm. I feel myself about to ride the wave of womanly emotion.

"Before I gave you some ass, it was always, 'Denise, can I stay or Denise, you should let me hit that.' But now that you have hit it a couple of times, you act like you don't give a shit about me."

"I act like I don't give a shit about you? Where'd you get that crazy-ass idea?"

"Where'd I get it? Where'd I get it?"

"Yes, Denise. How'd you come up with that one?"

"You're the one who walked out in the middle of an argument. Then you stay out all night and don't even call me to try to peace things up."

"I thought everything was cool when I left."

"Well, you thought wrong, nigga."

I throw his fifteen hundred dollars in his face and rush away, feeling like tears are about to fall from my eyes.

Mandingo

What type of crazy shit was that?

I guess Denise is just like every other woman who got a piece of this dark meat — strung the fuck out.

I'd better go check on her, though, to make sure she's OK.

I walk softly up the stairs and peak into her bedroom. There are rose petals everywhere and my senses tell me that Denise had had more than a few candles lit recently. Apparently, something was supposed to go down that I didn't think about.

As I look at Denise sitting on the bed in her see-through nightie, I put two and two together.

She must have been planning on us having an episode last night.

"Denise?"

"Go away," she says softly.

"No, Denise, you don't mean that. Can I come in, please?"

"It's a free country. You can do whatever you want."

"Maybe I can but not in your house. I'm not taking any

liberties I'm not offered. Now, again, can I come in?"

"Don't try to get all high seditty with me, Mandingo."

I look at her as if to say, "Come on now."

"Just bring your black ass in here."

I walk in and sit beside her on the bed. I start rubbing her arms and back.

"Can you tell me what's going on, please, Denise? I'm a little confused here."

"Nothing's going on."

I give her a look that says, "Bullshit."

"I guess I'm just tripping about Mrs. Goutier."

"Why? Is she here?"

She twists her face up so I continue.

"There are all these romantic hints so I thought maybe something didn't go down the way you wanted it to."

"Now you're being observant," she whispers under her breath but I still hear her.

"Denise, can you please tell me what's up?"

She sighs loudly then lets out a mouthful.

"I don't know what's up, OK? I'm confused. I think I'm feeling you, but I don't want to be feeling you. I don't want to lose my best friend, and I don't want to hear about you being with someone else."

"Are you jealous?"

"This is not a time for fucking jokes, Mandingo."

"I'm not joking." I'm lying my ass off. "I'm trying to be serious."

She gives me a look that indicates that she knows I'm lying my ass off.

"Look, Denise. I've been big on you for a minute. But

you've always pushed me away. I'm just not understanding what's going on with you right now. I'm just doing what you said and not getting caught up or even thinking that I'm gonna be able to have something serious with you."

"So, you just jump to the next bitch last night even though you fucked me the day before?"

"I don't know where all this is coming from."

"You're the one who acted like you're so big on me but it's pretty funny how you ain't thinking too much about me now that you have money in your pocket. You used to call me every day. You probably were just using my ass. I thought you cared about me."

I look at her strangely. I'm beyond confused. I'm not sure what I'm supposed to say right now.

"Say something, nigga."

She pushes the issue. That doesn't help because I'm mad confused.

"OK, Denise. I don't know what you want me to say. But prior to our argument last night, I told you repeatedly how much I love you."

"I didn't believe you."

"Well, I know how I feel. But let's just say that I was lying. At least I cared enough to want you to think that I love you. You've never given me that much."

"Nigga, you can't tell how I feel about you? Haven't I shown you?"

"I know what you've shown me but that doesn't matter. You've never professed your love to me. You've never tried to lock me down. The closest you've ever gotten was telling me you've got love for me after I told you that I love you."

"Because I do have love for you."

"That's not really the same thing as saying I love you."

"So that's why you're dogging me?"

"I never said I was dogging you, and I don't know what makes you think I am."

She rolls her neck then her eyes.

"See, here's the thing. Most women don't want to tell a man that they love him first because they think that the words will open up the possibility to them getting hurt. Then a lot of women don't want to say it at all because they know they'll be hurt. They come up with this 'I got love for you' shit to protect their own hearts. But 'I got love for you' translated from woman speak means 'I love you' — probably in most cases. And the probably in most cases part is where it gets too hard. If I'm opening up my heart to you with either a definite or a lie by saying 'I love you,' then I want you to open up your heart to me in the same way if you feel the same way. I'm not gonna be all open and vulnerable while you're protecting yourself. Fuck that. So unless I hear certain shit from you, I know we're cool and neither one of us owes the other a thing. At the least, I don't have to worry about being wrong when I think you love me over you saying the 'I got love for you' bullshit. I think that you and I are both protecting ourselves and I don't see anything wrong with that."

"Everything you just said proves that you don't understand me."

"Maybe not fully. But I don't claim to. In a way, I don't even try to. I ask you specific questions trying to get you to shed light on what I don't understand. It's up to you to answer or not. If you don't answer them, it's harder for me to truly understand you. I'm cool with that lack of total understanding as long as you and I remain cool and as long as you're cool with me not totally understanding you. I just need you to know that you have a certain responsibility to me understanding you."

"Amazing."

"What's amazing?"

"You've just found a way to blame me for your not being able to understand me and all the things I go through."

"This is not a blame thing..."

"Well, that's what you're doing."

"No. That's not what I'm doing. I'm saying that throughout my entire life, I've been told that if you don't understand something you need to ask questions. So my question to you is, am I supposed to magically understand something when I never get an answer? And 'I'm not gonna answer that' is not an answer that's gonna help me become enlightened about something that I'm lost about."

"Now you're just being a smart ass."

"I'm not trying to be funny. I'm trying to be thorough. I just want to make sure that we don't damage our friendship. You mean too much to me."

"We're alright. I'm just upset with you right now."

"And I'm trying to come up with a way so you can stop being upset with me."

"Don't even waste your time. It's just gonna take me a while. So let's just change the subject. Let me tell you why I called you."

I pause before telling him the business reason why I called. No, it's not a lie. But the truth is that I'm feeling real big on him right now, and that's what I wanted to tell him last night, before my woman's intuition told me that he had been with someone else.

"Basically, Mandingo, my phone was ringing off the hook last night after you left. Everyone wants a piece of you. You're the next big thing. You're every woman's fantasy and every man's nightmare. No man can compete with your considerable assets. You have clients and clients set up for days—black, white, Hispanic, even Chinese. Our pockets are about to be laced! I hope you're happy."

I start tearing up and I'm not sure why. I guess the thought of Mandingo with a variety of women is affecting me in a way I didn't know possible.

I jump off the bed, run into the bathroom and lock the door so that I can cry in peace.

"Come on, Denise," he says, running after me. "Open the door. Let's talk about this. You know I'm here for you."

I don't say a word. I just sit on the toilet drowning in my own misery.

After a while, I start to feel better and realize that I can't stay in the bathroom forever. I have to get it together and do so quickly.

I hop up and look in the mirror. I wipe away the tears and splash cold water on my face. When I finish, I breathe heavily. I know full well what I have to do. My only option is to play a bit with Mandingo's head. In our ever-evolving struggle for power, he can't ever think that he's in control.

Well here goes nothing, I say to myself as I grip the doorknob and prepare to to put on the performance of my life.

CHAPTER FOURTEEN

Denise

I feel like such an ass. I should never have opened my mouth and in turn, my heart.

Sometimes, though, I have to go places I know I shouldn't go. All that needs to happen is for me to feel like someone's playing me for a fool and I lose it. This time, though, instead of just losing my mind, I lost much more. I lost all the power I'd built up with Mandingo. Now the cards are in his hands. There's only one thing left for me to do. Act like it never happened.

*****

"I apologize for fucking your brains out, Mandingo, and then for asking you to leave. That wasn't right of me."

"You didn't ask me to leave. I was leaving anyway."

"Damn. I must have really hurt you. You're acting like it never happened. Seriously, though, you're my best friend and

I didn't mean to hurt you."

Mandingo looks at me as if I'm tripping.

"No. I'm not tripping. I'm about to make you think that you're tripping."

"I really am sorry, Mandingo. So, will you please accept my apology?" He doesn't say anything. "Please?"

"What am I accepting your apology for again?"

"OK, if you want to be like that, then be like that. I was just trying to spare your feelings, that's all."

"Spare my feelings?"

"Can we change the subject?"

"Maybe we should because I'm lost."

"Don't worry about it. We can deal with it some other time if we decide to deal with it at all. If you're cool then it's not that important."

"But, a minute ago..."

"Mandingo, it's not that important. Can we move on?"

"I guess."

He looks at me like I'm nutty as a fruitcake. I make a mental note that pretending to act like an ass never happened is at least partially effective. Mandingo looks like he doesn't know if he's coming or going.

"So, Mandingo, the reason that I called you is I got a call from Mrs. Goutier last night. I planned to surprise you with the details but you never called me last night."

"You could have called me. You called me this morning."

"The phrase of the day is move on, Mandingo, move on."

"Whatever."

"Can I continue?"

"You're really trippin' now."

"Can I continue?"

He shakes his head up and down so I finish telling him.

"Mrs. Goutier says that she's never had as many orgasms as she's had with both you and me. She says she's been racking her brains trying to figure out who pleased her more, you or me, but she can't. So rather than continuing to drive herself crazy, she's decided to have both of us at the same time. That is, if both of us agree. She says she'll pay us handsomely."

Mandingo's eyes light up.

"So she wants to have a threesome with you and me?"

"That's what she says. I told her that I was down but that I had to ask you first. So now I'm asking you. What should I tell her?"

"Well, first of all, I'd like to know what she means by 'pay us handsomely'."

I roll my eyes.

"You don't have to worry about that. You're in the big leagues now. You should already know that Mrs. Goutier pays well. And her tips are off the chain. The more you make her come, the more she tips."

"So how am I supposed to know how much of her tip belongs to me for making her come and how much will belong to you?"

"I hope I haven't created a monster. Your arrogance is starting to irk the shit out of me."

"I can't help it that I get the job done."

"Sweetie, do I have to remind you that the first time I tested you out you didn't get the job done. I had to school you on how to give it to a woman the way she wants you to give it to her. You were fucking clueless."

"You helped me to do you better but you can't take all the credit."

"Whatever. Are you gonna do the thing with her or not?"

"I guess so. When is it supposed to go down?"

"Her husband gets back in town tomorrow evening so she wants to do it today or first thing in the morning."

"Can we do it first thing in the morning?"

"Why can't you do it today?"

"I'm not saying that I can't. I'm saying that I'd rather do it first thing in the morning."

"Nigga, I'm trying to get at this money as fast as I can. Don't become complacent because you have a couple dollars in your pocket."

"Nah. It's not that. You're right. I owe you a lot and I'll never be able to pay you back unless I start making money on the regular."

"Who said anything about you owing me money?"

"You did. Maybe not just now, but you did."

I feel myself getting angry again.

"Well, we're not talking about you paying me back money right now. We're talking about you not making me miss out on money."

"I feel you. Seriously, though. I told my aunt I'd help her with something today so I don't want her to think I'm playing her out."

"You can't just help her out tomorrow?"

"My uncle always comes around on Sundays and I don't want to run into him. You know he always makes me upset."

"Well, damn! Can you do it on Monday? This is a lot of

money we're talking about here."

"Can I at least call her and ask her?"

"Alright but hurry up. Don't fuck this up for me, Mandingo."

Mandingo

I call Aunt Kadija and try to talk in code so she doesn't know what's really going down.

"Hey, Auntie. I was gonna try to come back later but I wanted to know how late is too late? I might have to do something for my job."

"I'm glad you want to come back, baby. It doesn't really matter. You can stay the night if you want. Your uncle doesn't normally get here until late in the afternoon, anyway, even though I always ask him to come earlier."

"Cool. So I'll call you when I'm on my way. It may be late, though."

"Well, at least you had the decency to ask ahead of time. You're nothing like your uncle, Mandingo. Just come. You don't have to call. Oh yeah. And remind me to give you your key when you get here. I ran out and had one made after you left."

"OK, Auntie. I will."

Whoa. My shit is potent!

"So, what are you gonna do, Mandingo?"

"I'll do it. I just want to do it as fast as possible. I don't want to be waking up my aunt too late at night."

"I don't see why your uncle can't step up. It's his wife."

"Mind yours, Denise. Mind yours."

"The only reason I'm being accommodating is because it's your family. Don't think I'm backing down for any other reason."

"Trust me. You're the last person I'd think would ever back down."

"Well, as long as you know."

CHAPTER FIFTEEN

Denise

I'm not really sure what's going on with Mandingo, but I don't care. I'm about to get some of his good dick, and he won't even be thinking that it's anything other than business.

Plus, I'm about to taste Mrs. Goutier's sweet pussy again. Today is gonna be crazy special.

*****

We arrive at Mrs. Goutier's and she directs us to the guest-house in the back.

"I never even knew she had a guesthouse," I say.

I get upset momentarily because she never invited me to this small paradise despite the numerous trysts we've had. And Mandingo's only serviced her once!

I'm trying to maintain my professionalism even though I'm pissed. But the truth of the matter is that the more I sit in the lap of luxury, the better I start to feel.

"Make yourselves at home," Mrs. Goutier tells us. "I'm about to get more comfortable."

She switches away with her plump ass bouncing from side to side.

I'm about to have the time of my life.

*****

Mandingo and I survey the guesthouse. It truthfully is a small paradise. There are twin Jacuzzis facing each other at a ninety degree angle from two gigantic marble statues of lions. Spouting from each of the the lions' mouths, between what appears to be eighteen carat gold teeth, is a liquid that can't be water because it's too dark. Upon further inspection, we discover that its Crystal.

"Goddamn! This place is banging!"

Cemented into the ground every few feet are marble mini-bars with Mrs. Goutier's patented top shelf stock.

Mandingo and I don't wait a second to indulge.

He has a Grey Goose and Cranberry and I have a Moet mimosa. I totally ignore Mandingo when he tells me not to open her bottle of Moet. This bitch has money hand over fist. I'm sure she's not gonna miss one bottle, or even a small portion of a bottle.

****

"What's up kiddies?" Mrs. Goutier asks when she rejoins us.

She has on a stunning, shimmering negligee.

Her breasts look like they're about to bust out of the top,

her waist is as small as when she was a teenager, and her ass is to die for. I'm getting turned on just looking at her.

Funny thing, though, Mandingo looks like he's not beat at all. Now, I know I can't make a generalized statement about him because he's a man and all women think men are sitting around all the time thinking about having a threesome. But I can say that Mandingo has thought about it on numerous occasions because I know him personally and he's told me so. That's why it's so curious to me that he isn't dancing a jig right now. Hell, his ass should be break dancing or something. But it's not. He's just as calm and reserved as he wants to be.

"So Mandingo, are you ready to join the party?" I ask him, trying to break him out of whatever funk he's in. I know he's had a rough time lately but he has to keep his personal family shit at home. We're conducting some real serious business right now.

"Yeah. I'm ready when y'all are. But to tell you the truth, I was hoping I could watch y'all get the party started before I join in."

"Just like a man. I won't complain if Mrs. Goutier doesn't. That's exactly what I want anyway."

I follow her lead as she heads into what I thought was the only dark corner in the guesthouse. It turns out, though, that the darkness leads into a smaller room. When Mrs. Goutier flips a switch, I hear a flickering sound and dozens of candles simultaneously come to life around the room.

In plain view is a large, luxurious bed with Mrs. Goutier's patented mirrors on the ceiling.

We sink into the bed which is so soft I feel like I'm losing myself in a sea of quicksand. The mattress magically conforms to the contours of our bodies.

At first, I wasn't feeling Mandingo but now I think the way that he's hiding in the corner peaking at us is sexy and mysterious. It seems as if as soon as we forget about him and get caught up in our own thing, he's gonna appear from out of nowhere.

I put him out of my mind momentarily and start to suck on Mrs. Goutier's neck. I've missed her. Goddamn, I've missed her.

Her neck tastes like a strawberry and cream Lifesaver. It's fruity and luscious and delicious. What a pleasure it is to be back home again.

While I'm licking and sucking Mrs. Goutier's neck, she reaches down and starts rubbing my pussy through my sweatpants.

"Don't you want to take those off?" she asks while blowing in my ear.

"If you want them off, bitch, take them off." I'm all ready to play her game.

"So that's how you want to play, huh?" she asks me before grabbing and squeezing my ass.

I remember how much I loved the cat and mouse game she and I used to play.

She undoes the string on my sweatpants and slowly and sensuously pulls them down. Before long, her lips and tongue are tracing a trail from my stomach to my calves and all parts in between, over and over. I can't help but shiver. She does me exactly the way I love to be done.

Mandingo

I watch as ass on ass and tits on tits have their way with one another. Separately, they are both bombshells. Collectively, they are a dream come true. They are a fantasy that can't be paralleled.

Mrs. Goutier's ass looks heavenly as she winds it in the air while she's licking Denise's pussy. The black/white bitch thing would give any man a heart attack. She definitely gets my engine running.

But she's not Denise and she's definitely not Aunt Kadija. Aside from her masterful skills at sucking dick, she's not even Karen Steinberg.

When it becomes apparent that Denise is about to climax, I tiptoe behind Mrs. Goutier and grab her waist roughly, pushing my tongue into her pussy.

She jerks in ecstasy and surprise.

I lick her pussy, and I'm once again amazed at her taste. I feel like I'm dining at the Cheesecake Factory.

She wiggles her ass and pushes it back into my face. Suddenly, I get really caught up in her ass. I want it. Not because of anything other than I want to hear her scream.

I move my tongue from her pussy to her asshole. I lick her up and down until I feel she's in unison with me, wiggling her ass just as she was when I was licking her pussy.

Once I feel like she's ready for it, I pull down my zipper and release half of my dick through the hole in my boxers. I know that even half of my shit will have her running for the hills.

I don't give her the opportunity to figure out what I'm

about to do. I stand up and quickly stick the head of my dick in the place that my tongue has just vacated.

She gasps.

I push in half inch to an inch at a time until I feel like she can't take anymore. Then I start stroking her ass in and out with my dick while I'm squeezing her little-ass waist. I'm contemplating if I'm gonna give her more than half or not. But I never get the chance to make the decision because Denise gets up and decides to switch as soon as Mrs. Goutier starts moaning like she's losing control.

I guess Denise wasn't lying about being jealous when it comes to her. That's cool, though. I wasn't really trying to be fucking Mrs. Goutier all night long. I will run up in Denise, though.

As soon as Denise kneels down on top of Mrs. Goutier, I position myself behind her. I might be wrong but it seems like she braces herself as if she knows what's about to go down.

Initially, I rub on Denise's ass and stick my middle and index finger in and out of her pussy. But once I hear Mrs. Goutier get back into her rhythm, I decide it's OK to go further with Denise.

I ram my dick into her already dripping wet pussy. I decide to dismiss her lessons about taking it easy with a woman.

Every woman wants to be fucked for real from time to time.

This is one of those times. I decide to give it to Denise rough, rugged and raw. I treat her like my dick is a shot of hard liquor that I want her to take straight up with no chaser.

I can tell that I'm killing her by the way that she's moaning. Even though she's pumping back on my dick as I'm ramming it into her pussy, I think she's only doing it to save face. She doesn't want me to know that she really can't handle all of this dark meat.

Although I'm tearing into Denise's pussy, I realize that I forgot for a second how good her shit is. It's the perfect combination of tight and wet that makes a man just want to bust with the quickness. I slow down my stroke a little but I think she notices the crack in my armor.

Denise starts throwing her ass back at me wildly. I can't even describe the circling motion she's doing, or even how she's doing it. All I know is that she's giving me her pussy in a real serious way. In an instant, she's reminding me that she may not be Aunt Kadija, but her fuck game is no joke either. As a matter of fact, I've never lasted as long with Denise as I have with Aunt Kadija. And tonight won't be any different. Around ten or fifteen minutes after putting my dick in her pussy, I feel myself tensing up. In an instant, I'm grabbing her around her waist and releasing my semen into her pussy.

Denise's pussy is just too damned good.

CHAPTER SIXTEEN

Mandingo

It's almost eleven when we leave Mrs. Goutier and nearly midnight when I leave Denise.

I'm happy because I'm over ten thousand dollars richer and also because I managed to go through the entire ordeal with giving Mrs. Goutier only about a half hour of the dick.

Denise seems to be satisfied as well. I guess my shot made her feel a lot better than she was feeling before. Lack of good dick can make the most chipper woman a real bitch.

I'm glad I told Denise that I had to help my aunt tonight. She didn't even put up a fuss when I jumped in the shower or when I was about to leave. I guess half-hearted honesty can get you somewhere. I do have to do something for my aunt. It's just nothing near what Denise might think it is.

*****

Aunt Kadija looks heavenly when she opens the door.

She has on a terry cloth robe that's sticking to her body and her skin is dripping wet. She'd obviously just gotten out of the shower and come downstairs when she heard me at the door.

She grabs me and kisses me on the mouth as if we've been kickin' it for years. She's totally natural with me, just as I feel one hundred percent at ease with her.

"How was work?" she asks.

"Same ole, same ole." Work is the last thing I want to talk about with her.

We stand and share a moment of awkwardness until Aunt Kadija finally decides to finish drying herself.

"Well, have a seat and make yourself at home." She pauses and starts up the stairs. "I'll be right down when I finish or you can come up and wait for me."

"No. Go ahead and take your time. But do you have anything to eat? I'm starving."

She pauses on the stairs.

"I said to make yourself at home. Why don't you just go look in the kitchen?"

I am so distracted by how sexy she looks on the stairs with her hair soaking wet and her skin glistening with drops of water that I almost forget for a moment that my stomach is growling. And it doesn't help that her bald pussy is peeking out the opening of her robe. Yet my stomach is telling me its time to stop kidding myself about having the energy to play house with Aunt Kadija. I have to go feed it.

"OK. I'll check things out in the kitchen."

"Good. I'm sure you won't be disappointed, baby."

She gives me the sexiest, most caring look before turning

and continuing up the stairs.

Why isn't Uncle Moriba here all the time, all day, every day?

*****

In the kitchen, I find a meal fit for a king. My aunt has made me an enormous Porterhouse steak, garlic mashed potatoes, creamed spinach and peach cobbler wrapped in plastic with a note stating, "Eat me, Mandingo. You're gonna need all the energy you can get."

A childlike smile fills my face. I'm probably blushing, too. Whatever the case, I'm happy as hell right now.

I put the plate in the microwave and press the minute button twice. While I'm waiting for my dinner to heat up, I grab a cup and open the refrigerator. I can't believe my eyes.

Staring me in the face is a bottle of Moet with a sign taped to it that says, "Mandingo's champagne."

I grab the bottle and open it. As I throw the cork in the trash, I hear the microwave chirp three times to let me know it's finished doing it's magic.

*****

I'm sitting on the couch, stuffed and with a slight buzz after drinking half a bottle of Moet.

Like an angel, Kadija floats back down the stairs wearing a long, slinky, see-through white robe. The sheer fabric clings seductively to her titties and pussy mound. My manhood starts to rise and my mouth starts to water. I can't wait for her to come close to me. I have to touch her. I have to feel her.

And Jah knows I want to taste every inch of her.

When she's finally standing over me, I slide my hands under her robe and rub her smooth skin. I practically fall off the chair, my mouth leading the way to her calves and thighs. I start kissing them softly and work my way south. I lift one of her legs so I can suck on her foot and in doing so, notice her delectable pussy staring at me.

Don't worry. You'll get your chance.

I lick and suck and torture Kadija's delightful creamy center for a long while. I love tasting her, and I marvel at how her sweet juices have pooled at the bottom of my chin. I know I've done a good job.

When she finally can't take any more foreplay, she pushes me away with all her might and lays on the couch. I can see she's tingling and shaking. I've taken her to that place.

She regaining her composure and pulls me in front of her. She takes the tip of my thick dick in her mouth and sucks it. Then she grabs my ass and pushes me deeper into her mouth until I feel the back of her throat.

"Suck this dick," I tell her, my accent more prevalent. I feel like I'm back in my homeland. She's pleasing the hell out of me right now.

I manage to open an eye and look down at her. Her wetness is glistening between her legs and dripping down her thighs. That's all that I need to see. She's as ready for me as I am for her.

I grab her shoulders and push her back. She gasps for air when my dick pops out her mouth.

She gasps again when I push myself inside of her. The pain/pleasure look on her face reinforces my knowledge that she's never been with anyone as big as me.

"Oh, Mandingo. That dick is so big. Please give it to me, baby. Give it to me!"

Her cries of passion are all the encouragement I need to shove as much of myself inside of her as I can.

"Oh shit!" she screams in agony as she weakly pushes at my thighs as if she can't handle as much as I'm giving her.

"No. Take all of me, baby. You want me, so take me."

"Okay, baby," she says barely above a whisper. "Take your pussy. It's yours, so take it."

I arch my back and rearrange myself on my knees to get more leverage so I can give her this dick like I want to. With each thrust, she moans her approval. I wouldn't give away the feeling for my life.

"Mandingo, yes, take your pussy. Take your pussy, baby. Yes, Mandingo, fuck your pussy!"

She's shouting so loud, it mesmerizes me and I'm so totally into what I'm doing, that I don't hear the front door open.

Then I vaguely hear Uncle Moriba shout, "What the fuck is going on?"

But I'm trapped in ecstasy. It must be a dream.

Reality strikes, though, when I feel pain against my cheek. My eyes fly open and I'm looking up at my uncle. He's standing over me about to stomp my chest with his foot.

In the nick of time, I grab his foot and he falls to the floor.

Kadija is screaming. "Don't touch him, Moriba! You had your chance and you didn't take it. Just leave. You can't stop me from moving on."

"You little bitch!" he shouts and lunges at her.

I cut him off with a right cross that connects to his chin

and he stumbles backwards.

"You would hit your uncle?" he asks, stunned "You'd defile our family like this?"

He gets up and backs away from me slowly. He stops at the door and stares me down.

"You are dead to me, Mandingo, totally dead. You have dishonored our family and shamed us in the sight of Allah."

And with that, he's gone.

I help Kadija pick up the pieces of her living room. Yet I'm not sure if I'll be able to pick up all the other broken pieces, though — of myself and of Kadija. That's gonna be a project that will take some time.

CHAPTER SEVENTEEN

Mandingo

Six weeks later

Denise didn't lie. Servicing Mrs. Goutier properly has led more and more clientele to me. Over the past three weeks, I've knocked the back out of the wives of some of the top movers and shakers in the political and business arena. New York City would turn topsy turvy if it knew that an African immigrant on a student visa was serving up large helpings of meat to their precious white hussies.

My reach saw no boundaries. Wives of city hall cabinet members, police department lieutenants and captains, and even prominent officials themselves like the blond-haired, blue-eyed bombshell newbie Assistant District Attorney two weeks ago, I was fucking early and often. And the measly little bank account I started has swollen to over six figures in a little more than a month. In fact, I bought a safe and put it in my apartment in the Village just to stash my money. I didn't want the authorities getting suspicious about how I was raking in so much dough so fast.

Things have gotten so good, Denise and I have even created a business called Mandingo, Inc. We started a pay phone service, 1-900-MANDINGO, where after successfully punching in a secret password and answering a series of questions, a customer can then order their fantasy.

You would think that Denise would be happy with business booming and all, yet she's far from thrilled. I've fucked some of everybody over the past six weeks but she hasn't been one of them. I've been keeping everything with us business as usual. We've remained the best of friends, but I can tell that she wants more.

How can Denise blame me, though? She's sent me mixed signals right from the beginning. I was real big on her real fast and when I told her so she was like, "Whoa, whoa, whoa...slow your roll, partner."

So when Kadija came at me and didn't mind that I started feeling her, I appreciated her up-front, no game play attitude. I look at it like a lesson to Denise. If you want someone, let it be known, just as they're letting it be known. Playing games can leave you on the sidelines — where Denise now is. I'm not sure what's going to happen with Kadija but I'm reserving my energy for her. Denise will just have to be on standby.

With all that being said, it hasn't been easy for me to see Kadija. Uncle Moriba is stalking both of us. I've had my cell phone number changed three times since the night he saw me fucking the shit out of his wife. She's changed her number twice as well. She's also had the locks changed and the security system transferred over to a new company just to keep

Uncle Moriba out. She's also filed a restraining order against him. I guess a fine-ass woman who steps off from a man who didn't appreciate what he had when he had it has to go through a bunch of bullshit. It's a sad, sad situation. But it's always best to get totally free of someone who's not worth the time of day.

Another reason I haven't had time for Denise is that I've been servicing another of my uncle's wives, his pride and joy, Fateema. And she's paying me.

I guess he mouthed his displeasure to her one day, and she felt like I must have been something special considering how big Kadija had been on my uncle. And I'm sure she felt like a second choice after Kadija excused herself from the running. Bottom line, she didn't want her competition ending up with something that she couldn't have. So she paid me top dollar to make sure that didn't happen.

Besides my surprise at seeing her standing at my peephole, I couldn't figure out how she found out where I lived in the first place.

"Are you gonna let me in or are you gonna keep staring at me from that damned peephole?" she asked. "I know your ass is in there."

I let her in.

"Word around town is that you're the man to see for some really, really good dick," she shocked me by saying. "So I'm here so my little nephew can hook me up. Can a sister get your platinum service?"

"Aunt Fateema, what are you talking about?" I asked.

"Boy, you know good and well what I'm talking about. I need some good dick and you have it so let's get this show on the road."

"You're my aunt!"

"Don't try to play me, Mandingo. I know you fucked Kadija. Now tell me you don't want to fuck with this."

That's when she pulled up her tee-shirt to show me she wasn't wearing a bra. She had both Denise and Mrs. Goutier beat with her perfect titties. And with her pretty face and tiny waist, I wanted her as quickly as I saw her goods.

I know it was wrong, but I'm a man. What do you expect me to do?

"This should be good," she said when she handed me five thousand of my uncle's hard earned dollars.

She closed the door behind her and continued to undress. I remember thinking that I'd never seen such a picture of perfection. It was as if Michelangelo had sculpted her body inch by inch. I had to have her.

I didn't waste time with words. I knelt before her and started licking her pussy.

"You don't waste any time, do you?" she asked in between moans.

"No, not normally," I said. "But do you think you're gonna be able to handle what I'm serving up? Your pussy seems too tiny to take a real man."

"You just let me handle that. I need to get it worked out. Just give me what I paid for."

She was talking slick to the wrong nigga. Yes, she was my aunt. And yes, I had fantasized about making love to her on many occasions. But at that moment, with her naked body in front of me and her sweet pussy juices all over my face, I had to make her eat her big words. And it didn't take long before

I made her do just that.

I shoved my fingers into her mouth while I was still eating her out. The way she sucked them made me think that she was wishing it was my dick in her mouth and not my fingers. So I obliged her.

"Come suck this big, black dick."

It was as if Fateema had created the art of dick sucking herself when she put me in her mouth. She stared up into my eyes while she took me deeper into her small mouth than any woman had ever done before. She even beat out Mrs. Goutier and I had thought that it should have been illegal for someone to suck dick as good as she did.

Fateema stopped short of making me come and knelt on top of me and placed my dick inside of her.

"Umph," she had moaned.

I could tell that she had bitten off a little bit more than she could possibly chew.

"Gosh, my gosh," she moaned. "This dick is good. Oh yes, it's so damned good."

She rode me for an eternity but she slowed her grinds and thrusts every time I got close to coming.

"I want more of this good dick," she said. "I don't ever want you to come."

My dick had started to pulsate and was in pain from holding back the orgasm we'd been flirting with for so long. I had to do something about it so I'd decided to change position.

"Turn around so I can see that big ass," I said.

"No. You're too big," she replied.

"Didn't you say you wanted your money's worth?" I asked her. "Turn around so I can really give you this dick.

She apprehensively followed my instructions. I can't tell you how perfect her phat ass and tight pussy looked to me from the back. I shoved myself inside her pussy and watched as fluids spewed out in long, thick spurts.

It seemed as if every nerve in her body was convulsing — or maybe doing the Harlem shake. The sweet and sexy voice she normally tried to hide so she wasn't taken as a pushover sounded heavenly to me. It turned me on that much more.

"Oh God, Mandingo. Oh God," she swooned barely above a whisper.

It was all I could handle. Before I knew it, I'd come in her pussy without wearing a rubber. And I'm sorry I did.

It was the first time and shit happens. But I'm sorry I did because after that first time, she demanded I come inside her pussy every time. Yes, it feels good but you can't continue to battle nature and win.

I guess it's my fault. But truth be told, her pussy's so good that her discount gets better and better.

The first time she gave me five grand but the last time we did it, she gave me only twenty-one hundred. Pretty soon it will be a serving of her famous fish casserole and dessert if I don't watch myself. I can't let good pussy fuck up business just because it's good pussy. I have to keep my eye on the prize. And I have to remember that it's Kadija who really wants me. I need to concentrate my efforts on the woman who really knows how to treat a man like a man.

I know we're meant to be. I just have to stay one step ahead of Uncle Moriba. In the end, Kadija will be mine. And his dream of having a slew of wives will be just as dead as his relationship with Kadija.

CHAPTER EIGHTEEN

Moriba

I don't know what makes Mandingo and Kadija think I'm gonna just back off and let them continue to do what they're doing. She made vows to me to the death. So whatever it is she's doing with him is only temporary. Allah has given me papers on her, and I will make her live up to her commitment to me.

I can't believe she's putting me through this. Kadija was supposed to be the one person I could count on. No one's loved me the way she's loved me.

But I really should have told her that no one's loved me the way she has. Kadija and I are meant to be together forever.

I haven't slept much since everything went down. I've sat in my car outside her house for hours on end. I've tracked her through the Onstar system I had secretly installed in her car. Kadija cannot hide from me. I'm her husband and I'll continue to keep tabs on her. There's no law in the world that can stop me.

It doesn't matter that I've had to go to court for a silly restraining order. Hell, I've even spent a couple days in jail for violating it. But sooner or later, they'll realize that she's my wife and they don't have the right to tell me that I can't be around her. I will see her whenever I damned well please and things would be much easier if everyone would realize that's how it's gonna be.

*****

Things with Fateema haven't been as sparkling as usual either and I've been seeing her more often now. She's developed some type of attitude and doesn't want to have sex with me as much.

Yes, I know that she was just giving it to me once a week for a while. But she should welcome the fact that I'm not spending as much time or money with Kadija. I'll never understand why women are the way they are when they have a good man at their side to take care of them.

*****

Now, Mandingo, he's another story. I don't know what makes him think he's gonna get away with what he's doing to me.

But I got a plan to make his life miserable. He can't get away with what he did to me. I'm family. I don't know what the hell's come over him. But I do know he was barking up the wrong damned tree when he decided to come for me. He should have known that I'm not what he wants. I guess he'll just have to find out the hard way the difference between a small timer like himself and a heavyweight like me. His life is pretty much in ruins now. He just doesn't know it yet.

CHAPTER NINETEEN

Mandingo

I haven't seen Kadija in a couple of days and I can't wait any longer. Of course Denise tried to convince me to mind my business and stay with her. I don't know why I told her about the trouble my aunt and uncle were having, but I did.

I didn't come completely clean, though. I painted the picture of how their relationship is falling apart and how my aunt has no one to turn to but me.

Denise still feels like it's not my place.

"You should just mind your own business with this one, Mandingo," she keeps telling me.

But wild horses couldn't keep me away from Kadija today. Not in a million years.

*****

I feel the hood of her car like I've been doing since the debacle at her house with Uncle Moriba. It's odd that it's as cold as winter.

I thought she said she was running out to the store to pick up a few things to make me a dinner fit for a king.

I go inside and call her name several times but I don't hear anything. Perplexed, I walk up the stairs to the bedroom but still don't see her. Next I check the bathroom but she isn't anywhere to be found.

I slowly walk downstairs while putting my thinking cap on, wondering where she could be. I pause at the bottom of the stairs and smile as I look at the kitchen door.

She's playing games with me. Now I know where she's at.

I tiptoe over to the door and push hard. I trip over something and fall hard but not on the floor. Something lessens my impact.

When I catch my bearings, I see that it's Kadija all bloodied up and her blood is on my clothes as well.

Before I get a chance to think clearly, I hear banging at the front door.

"Open up! New York City Police! Open the door, now!"

Of course I open the door and try to explain to them what happened. But before I know it, my face is pressed against the carpet and I'm in handcuffs.

These idiots think that I did this to her. I could never hurt her.

"You have the right to remain silent. Anything you say may be used against you in a court of law."

The sergeant looks like he's auditioning for a Ku Klux Klan rally and is extremely smug as he reads me my rights.

He searches my pockets while asking me if I have any weapons or anything else sharp. I'm barely paying him any mind. I'm in a daze about what's transpiring. But I do find a way to shake my head no.

"Mandingo, Inc. Hmm," he says, smirking, as he looks at my business card. "Well, those days are over now Mr. Businessman. Let's get your ass to the station house."

*****

I make my one phone call, and in a flash, Denise arrives at the station and raises pure hell. She has also brought with her one of the best attorneys in New York City. I guess she's not gonna let her bread and butter get sent up the river without a fight.

"I want to see him!" I hear her screaming. "I demand to see him right now. And y'all better not have laid a hand on him!"

"Relax, ma'am. He hasn't even been processed yet. You just have to wait while we go through normal procedures."

"You'd better make it quick," I hear the attorney say. "I'm sure the department doesn't want to put even more money in my bank account for choosing to violate this man's civil rights."

Rob Gineesmo, Esq. became famous several years ago when he stuck it to the city in a civil rights case to the tune of a ten million dollars.

Since then, he's taken on the cases of every major slime ball in the city, including some Mafia wise guys. To this day, he hasn't lost a single case. I feel more than secure now. But he isn't the only reason I feel secure. I'm not sure how, but Denise has found other ways to stack the deck.

She told me that the sergeant was tripping extra hard because he suspects that I've been servicing his wife. So he wants nothing more than to put me in jail and throw away the key.

And it was not only his wife. It was also his lieutenant's. Between the two of them, there is more than enough motivation to have my ass locked up for a long time.

But Denise tells me not to worry. At my arraignment, I find out why.

Conducting the case against me is the blue-eyed, blond-haired ADA I'd been with a while back. I spot her and smile. Not long ago, she didn't look as powerful as she does right now. She was being manhandled by me and loving it.

*****

Denise told me she liked role play and being controlled. So I gave her her money's worth.

"Come here you white bitch and suck this black dick," I demanded of her.

"Yes, sir," she said timidly before walking over to me.

"No. Don't walk. Crawl your ass over to me, you fucking slut. And don't take all day either."

She did exactly what I told her to do. Without uttering a word, she put my dick in her mouth and started going to town.

I couldn't believe this pretty, white bitch was sucking my dick. And she was paying me handsomely for the honor.

In addition to her sparkling eyes and silky hair, she had much more going for herself. She was prettier than Pamela Anderson, Angelina Jolie and Anna Nicole Smith combined.

She had lips like Angelina Jolie, a body like Anna Nicole Smith, and a face more refined than Pamela Anderson's, who I always thought was the most beautiful white chick around.

I took her picture while she was sucking my dick. It turned her on. With each flash, she sucked the dick harder and harder.

I squeezed her soft, supple titties while she sucked me and got more turned on as I watched her rub on her own pussy.

She was so fucking pretty that I wanted to stare in her face while I was fucking her so I had her ride my dick.

"Oh yeah, baby. Oh yeah. Fuck this cunt. Fuck this cunt," she swooned.

She was in ecstasy from the moment she stuck my dick in her pussy.

Me? I just felt honored. I'd never been with such a pretty white chick before. And she was riding the shit out of my dick. It was erotic as hell.

*****

She keeps cutting her eyes at me while we wait for the judge to enter chambers. I keep wondering if she would be able to convict someone who slapped her face with his dick not that long ago, giving her pearl necklaces and coming on her face.

I don't have to wonder long. The judge arrives and everyone stands up.

Mr. Gineesmo and the ADA approach the bench simultaneously and after a brief chat, return to their tables.

"So what say ye, Ms. Prosecutor?" the judge asks.

Before I know what has happened, she announces that

she's dismissing the charges against me due to lack of evidence. I don't hear exactly what she says. All I know is that I am free to go.

Without addressing me, the ADA puts a note in my lawyer's hand and checks me before walking away.

Gineesmo turns to me and shakes my hand in congratulations. I glance down at the folded piece of paper he has slipped into my palm. Written across it is *Mandingo.*

When I'm outside and free again, I read the note.

"Hi Mandingo. You know you owe me so I expect to be getting my pussy pounded later. You know where to find me. 8:30 PM, sharp. And don't be a second late."

"What's that?" Denise asks.

Without answering, I hand her the note.

"You'd better do it," Denise says. "It's good to have an Assistant District Attorney in your back pocket."

I'm glad she's not tripping about me fucking someone else. The mere thought makes me tear up.

"I can't believe Aunt Kadija is dead," I say, breaking down.

"It'll be alright, Mandingo," she assures me. "Whatever it takes, we'll find her killer.

All I can do is hope she's right. I vow to do whatever it takes to get to the bottom of everything. And I'm convinced that my search will probably start and end with Uncle Moriba.

CHAPTER TWENTY

Denise

I've been going through a really rough time lately. I feel like I'm losing both my best friend and the man I love. I'm a fool. I should have been honest with him.

I'll give him some time to get over his loss and then I'll be straight with him. I need him in my life. And I need him inside of me. He's the only man who can take me where I need to go.

"Let's go get something nice to eat," I tell Mandingo. "I'm sure they didn't give you anything too tasty in the New York City prison system."

"Jail, Denise, not prison."

"Well, that doesn't matter. I'm just trying to feed you. Now you know you like to eat."

"You're right about that. Thanks for being a good friend, Denise ."

I grab his hand and kiss him softly on the lips.

"I'll always be your friend, Mandingo," I tell him sincerely, looking in his eyes with all the care I can muster. "And any time you need me, I'll be right here. Anything. It doesn't matter."

"That's good to know, Denise."

"I love you, boo. Don't scare me like that. I don't even want to think that someone has the power to take you away from me."

I search Mandingo's eyes to see his reaction to my words. It may be an awkward situation and my timing may not be perfect but I finally found a way to say to him the words he's been wanting to hear. I just hope he realizes how true they are and doesn't think that I'm just pitying him. I need him in my life more than ever. I just hope it's not too late.

*****

I take Mandingo to his favorite African restaurant. We both order spicy chicken and gravy over rice even though the gravy's too spicy for me. I don't care, though. I'm out with the man I love and it feels like old times. True, he has his own money now and doesn't need me in that way, but hopefully he realizes that I have been there for him and that he needs me in other ways. It's always good to have someone in your life you can count on.

*****

It's been so long since Mandingo has stayed with me it's kind of hard to disguise my excitement. I've missed him so much.

He's just gotten back from taking care of the ADA. I don't

want to know about it so I don't ask. I'm just happy that he doesn't seem real tired.

I put his favorite music on the CD player and dim the lights and spark up his favorite scented candles. I want everything to be perfect. I can't make any mistakes tonight. In the end, I have to show him that no one will love him like I do.

"Would you like a drink, Mandingo?"

"Damn, Denise. You must have been reading my mind. You've been real on point tonight. What? Did I win the grand prize or something?"

"No. That's not it. You never know how important something is to you until it's gone. I can't believe you were almost convicted for some bullshit. There's no way in hell you could kill someone. I almost lost you and that was the scariest thought I've ever had."

I start crying and Mandingo rushes over to console me.

"It's OK, Denise. I'm still here. You don't have to worry about anything. You didn't lose me. I'm still here."

"Do you really mean that, Mandingo? I really do hope you mean that."

We share a soft, sweet kiss that sends chills up my spine. Then we kiss again and again, each kiss becoming more and more passionate.

"I've missed you so much, baby," I whisper softly in his ear.

"I've missed you too, Denise."

"I should have told you this a long time ago, Mandingo..."

"That's okay."

"No. Let me finish, baby. I love you. I really do love you.

And I've missed you like crazy."

The look in Mandingo's eyes tell me that I got to him. He lifts me up and carries me upstairs to the bedroom.

Slowly, we undress each other like it was the first time.

Once we're both naked, I stand over him and feed him my breasts as if I'm nursing him. He sucks on them softly and caringly, alternating from one to another so as not to make one jealous of the other.

It feels heavenly.

After feeding him my breasts, I kneel down between his legs and take him into my mouth, showing him how much I've missed him. I suck him with all of my might.

His moans of ecstasy encourage me to please him more and more. I become totally in tune with his manhood. I don't believe I've ever tasted anything better.

After taking him to the brink of coming, I pull away from him and try to jump on top. I need to feel him inside of me, but he's not ready yet. He has other plans.

He lays me back on the bed and crawls between my legs. He lifts my leg up and one by one sucks each toe like it's sweet candy before finally putting my entire foot in his mouth. I moan in ecstasy.

After sucking on both my feet like he hasn't eaten in days, his mouth starts its upward journey, kissing and sucking my calves, the fronts and backs of my knees, then my thighs.

He gently pecks on the outside of my thighs before expertly working his way inside. I'm virtually losing my mind. I'm shaking all over and I'm as wet as the ocean. He turns me on even more by licking up every drop of me.

Without any regard for the fact that I'm already about to

pass out, he starts kissing and sucking on my clitoris. His lips surround its entire mass and his tongue barely flicks against it. I'm not sure I'm able to contain myself.

When he starts licking it softly up and down and side to side, I arch my back and lift up into his face, grinding away as hard as I possibly can. He's brought me to the point of no control.

I come in spurts all over his face. I'm spent. I can't imagine being any more satisfied than I am right now.

Finally, thankfully, he lifts his face from between my legs and grants me a momentary reprieve. It doesn't last long. In the next instant, I feel his humongous manhood pushing open the lips that guard the entrance to my valley of love. With its huge width and girth, its entrance will not be denied.

I cringe when only half of it is inside of me. The mixture of pleasure and pain that I feel is incomparable to anything I've ever felt before. I'm so glad to have my lover and friend back in my life. I pray he never leaves me again.

*****

I wake up with my thighs sore as all hell. I'm not sure how I'm even able to stand.

Yet my sense of smell has taken over and I begin to wonder what's going on. So I head straight for the kitchen.

Mandingo is standing over the stove, hooking up a concoction that smells heavenly. He is not aware of my presence so I just stand there and check him out.

He's the picture of perfection.

I've always loved him as a friend. But watching the muscles in his back flex as he stands over the stove making me something to eat thrills my sore pussy. The moment he put his dick in me for the first time, I was hooked, completely in shambles. I was lost in love for life. All I can do now is pray with all of my heart that he feels the same. I'm not sure what I'd do without him.

*****

"What are you doing down here? I wanted to surprise you," he says when he finally senses my presence.

"I smelled something marvelous, so I got curious."

"Well, if you don't go lay down so I can serve you break-fast in bed, I'm gonna throw all of this in the trash."

"But what is it? I wanna see," I whine.

"I'm counting to ten."

"Mandingo, please."

"Ten...nine...eight..."

"Alright, already. I'll leave."

I walk away pouting though smiling from ear to ear.

Maybe, just maybe, my wish will come true.

CHAPTER TWENTY-ONE

Mandingo

I snuck out this morning and picked up some basa fish, the lightest, flakiest fish I've ever tasted, hominy grits, oranges, mozzarella, cheddar cheese, and brown organic eggs.

I'm preparing breakfast just the way my mother did back in my village. Tears come to my eyes as I remember the love she put into every meal she made for us.

Although the thought of her makes me sad, I hear her voice telling me that I'm not alone in the world.

"You have to trust, son, in order to receive the full blessings of Allah. There is no other way."

I told myself that I would stop holding Denise's fear against her and give her another chance. It's not like she doesn't deserve it. She's been everything to me. The least I can do is show her my appreciation by trying to do right by her.

I heard her sneak up behind me as I was squeezing the oranges for the orange juice. It's a big ego booster to know that someone as special as she is is behind me, checking me out.

I really do love her. I've just had to find my way.

I wonder, though, if it's fair to get fully involved with her when my mind is on Kadija. I'm in mourning. And just a few days ago I thought that she was the one for me above anyone else. How could that change so quickly? Aren't we all supposed to have just one soul mate? And if that's true, how can Denise be my soul mate when I felt like Kadija was?

Bang, bang, bang.

A loud thump at the door quickly brings me back to reality and out of my thoughts.

"Mandingo Fink, open up! This is the police. We know you're in there!"

"That's odd," I mumble to myself before walking towards the door.

Before I get there, Denise comes rushing down the stairs closing her bathrobe and lunges to the door before I get a chance. She snatches it open violently and starts screaming.

"You bastards had better stop harassing us! Mandingo was just released yesterday. He wasn't even indicted. He's a free man and you need to just leave him the hell alone."

"Back away from the door, ma'am, and calm down," the officer says nastily. "You can join him at the station if you'd like."

"What's this about?" I ask before Denise has a chance to respond.

I'm fuming but act like I have some sense. I know that one of us has to.

"There's new information about your case so you have to come with us," the officer says.

"Am I under arrest?" I ask.

"We're the ones asking questions here," he says.

"Well, sir, if I'm not under arrest, it's been nice talking to you but I really have to go now. I'm kind of busy."

"You'll go when we say you can go," the other officer says snidely. "Step away from the door. We'll follow you to get some clothes, unless you'd rather go the way you are."

I have on boxers and no shirt. I definitely don't want to go out like this. Still, I show them that I'm not ignorant of the law.

"Sir, you haven't answered my question," I haven't budged. "I asked if I was under arrest."

"Oh, we have a smart ass," the second officer says, forcing his way in.

I start pushing it closed and yell, "Sir, I have not authorized you to enter my home."

"Yeah, he's resisting, Charlie," the first officer says as he's drawing his weapon.

"Bullshit," Denise screams. "You have nothing on him and you know it. He can't resist being arrested when he hasn't been told why you want him to go with you."

"I've had just about enough of this," the second officer says while grabbing me to put the cuffs on. "Nobody told him to try and get physical with an officer of the law. You have a good day," he says to Denise as he walks me out the door.

"Don't worry, Denise," I yell behind me. "Just call Gineesmo. I'm about to get some of the city's money."

"I will baby," she says, her voice cracking. "And I'll be there as soon as I can."

*****

At the station, all the Jakes look victorious. Yet their celebration is short-lived once their captain walks into the squad room.

"Why is this man here?" she asks.

I can't believe this, I'm thinking. *That's the chick I fucked the shit out of last weekend.*

"Ma'am, he tried to get physical with us," says the first officer.

"I don't believe that," she said, shooting me a wink that no one else sees. "You all had better not be antagonizing this man. The next person who harasses him will have time off with no pay to sit home and think about it. Do I make myself clear?"

No one says a word.

"Do I make myself clear?" she yells again.

"Yes ma'am," everyone in the squad room answers.

"Now, take off those cuffs," she demands.

Officer number one quickly obliges.

"I'd tell one of you to give him a ride home but you've already shown me that you can't be trusted to uphold the law. So I will escort this man home myself. I'll be back shortly."

She mumbles some more expletives as she grabs me and leads me out of the room. Once again, I'm saved by a client. What can I say? Law enforcement chicks need love too.

*****

"Isn't this funny?" she says as she drives the squad car.

She allows me to sit in the front seat. And why not? I haven't done anything wrong.

"Well, it wasn't all that funny to me," I reply. "I was in the middle of breakfast and my friend and I weren't wearing all that much."

"Sounds kinky," she says with a devilish grin on her face.

Her name is Lisa Chamberlain, Captain Lisa Chamberlain, and I note how she looks like a white Halle Berry with sexy short hair, a pretty face and stunning figure.

I wonder what made her decide to become a policewoman.

"I have to make a quick stop," she says.

"Okay," I answer before going back to my thoughts.

Lisa refused to meet me at my place or to let me come to hers. Instead, she insisted on meeting me at a cheap motel.

I walked in and she was wearing a tight black leather bra and short set with matching high heel boots. She looked like she came straight from the pages of one of those kinky magazines, but I didn't complain. She looked hot and I was ready to let her sizzle all over me.

She teased me for what seemed like forever, rubbing my dick through my pants and allowing me to rub her through her clothes. It was an eternity before she let me guide one of her amazing breasts out of her leather bra. But trust me when I say it was well worth the wait.

She was a little shit talker, demanding from me what she wanted, which turned me on.

"Suck my tits," she cooed. "Suck 'em!"

Things got downright kinky after that and I loved it.

*****

It is getting darker. I shake my head clear and focus on my surroundings. Lisa has driven me into an old, beat-up garage. I think she wants something to go down right here, right now. Good. It'll give me new things to daydream about.

Although it's hard for me to protest about being with her sexy ass, I can't help but think about the mental state Denise will undoubtedly be in. She's probably at the precinct right now wondering where I'm at.

I look Lisa in the eyes and explain the situation.

"We don't have a lot of time, Lisa. My friend will probably be worried sick about me when she doesn't find me at the police station."

"Well, we better take advantage of what little time that we have then," she says, unphased.

I love a woman who knows what she wants and goes after it without hesitation.

She removes her uniform and once again I get to see how stunning her figure is.

"Goddamn," I say. "I don't know when they started making white girls like you but y'all are trying to put black girls out of business."

She smiles at the compliment. "You like all of this, don't you?"

"Hell, yeah," I say before jumping in her arms.

I kiss all over her neck, her face and her lips before once again sucking on her titties.

I'm not wearing much and it takes her no time to get me naked. She definitely does not want to waste time with foreplay today. She wants a quick fuck and in a hurry.

She pushes me back against the trunk of the car and starts going to town on my dick. She sucks me with so much pressure and expertise that surprisingly I come in her mouth in less than two minutes. Yet she doesn't release me. She continues to suck me after swallowing every drop of my come.

Once she's satisfied that my dick is not about to get soft, she bends over in front of me and guides me into her hole. She moans with pleasure once I'm inside her and starts screaming like a made woman while violently throwing her head from one side to the other, just as she did on our previous encounter.

"Fuck me you black, African! Fuck me!" she screams loud and often.

After a few minutes, she pulls herself away from me and grabs my hand, guiding me off of the car. She leans herself back on the spot I just vacated with her legs wide open.

"Put that big, black dick in this cunt and fuck me like a whore," she demands me.

Of course I quickly oblige her.

"You want this dick, Lisa?" I ask her. "You want this dick?"

"Yes! Fuck yes," she gasps. My dick is getting to her.

We're fucking so hard and violently that it doesn't surprise me that we both collapse in ecstasy, coming together after less than ten minutes. Spent, we try to catch our breath.

*****

Lisa hands me a wad of cash when she drops me off at

Denise's place.

"I know you don't work for free," she says.

"Thanks," I tell her, perplexed about the money. "I didn't know that this is what was going down."

"Well, it's good to know that you like my sex enough to give it away to me. But I'm just happy with the discount. Believe me, you deserve every dime. Your dick is the bomb diggity."

We both laugh at her attempt at ebonics.

"Seriously, though," she continues. "You might want to keep a low profile for a while. It seems like everybody who's anybody is out to get you. You don't want to make their day by letting it happen."

"You're not telling me anything I don't already know," I reply. "Lately, it's been one headache after another. I'll be alright, though. I have an excellent lawyer."

She grabs my hand.

"Trust me, sweetie, your lawyer is not enough. Just do yourself a favor and don't make any waves. Things will die down in time."

I shake my head, acknowledging that I hear her. Then she jumps into my arms and gives me a tight hug as if she's my mother sending me away and this may be the last time she ever sees me.

"Be careful, sweetie," she says before giving me one of the sweetest kisses I ever had. "Bye, bye."

I walk away from her with a painted on air of confidence. But deep down inside I'm nowhere near as in control as I appear to be. Her words and mannerisms tell me that I may be in some deeper shit than I originally thought, and I'm not so dumb that I'm ready to dismiss them.

I need to protect my ass and that's what I'm gonna do.

I meet Denise at the front door and tell her that I'm OK. But she storms out the door, frazzled, before I have a chance to go in.

We both look like we've seen ghosts.

CHAPTER TWENTY-TWO

Mandingo

Two months later

With everything I've been through this winter and early spring, it's amazing I'm still maintaining A averages in my classes. And no matter what, I plan to keep it that way.

That's why I've slowed down a bit lately. It's hard to totally stop doing what I'm doing given the types of connected people I've been servicing and how persistent they can be. But I've found a way to be more careful when I do decide to see a client.

Before anything goes down, they meet me at Zoodo. Now, how funny does it look when an older white woman walks into an African club in the Bronx? Who knows? But I don't give a shit. The cops want no part of the Bronx, even on a late night tip, so I know I won't be getting set up there. If a bitch wants some dick, that's where she has to meet me. I have to protect my interests — mainly my own ass.

Besides, I love Zoodo.

Zoodo is where everybody who's anybody in New York's African community hangs out and shows off. It's a virtual meeting place for all the affluent people of my culture.

Whenever I need to release some stress, I go there and listen to the sounds of DJ Khadafi. His blends always seem to take me where I need to go. I'm usually uptight when I first walk in the door but after listening to a few songs, I feel myself loosening up. After that, it's pretty much a wrap. I'm out dancing, whether or not I choose to find a beautiful vixen to be my partner.

Tonight I'm at Zoodo for a different reason. My Organizational Dynamics professor called me and said she had to talk to me about a recent quiz. I was paranoid as hell when she called because I thought that she might be working with the police to set me up. I told her that I had to come here tonight so that's the only way I could meet her. I was surprised as hell when she said it was cool.

My professor, Neve Richards, is a blond-haired, blue-eyed, all American girl. She's the type of white girl every southern redneck would lynch you for if they even caught your eyes dancing in her direction. To white men, she's hot and sexy and they all love her. Ask me, or any black or African man, and we'll tell you she looks sickly and anorexic. I just think she's crazy as hell for agreeing to meet me at Zoodo. I wonder what she wants.

Professor Richards walks into Zoodo looking the epitome of preppy. I try to be nonchalant but it's obvious I'm with her. Every black eye is on us. I just hope she's quick about whatever it is she has to say. I need to get out of here before my

face gets set in stone in everyone's memory banks. That's the
last thing I need right now.

*****

I lead her through the crowd and find as isolated a corner as
the always overcrowded club allows. We squeeze into a tiny
booth at the back of the club and I try to relax despite all the
eyes that are on me right now. I can't let this go on any longer
than it has to so I immediately cut to the chase.

"So, what seems to be the problem, Professor? I'm not
used to being out on a school night."

"Well, Mandingo, I had to let you know that your performance is slipping a little bit. I don't want you to be blind-
sided by a C when you live and die to get all A's. I'm making
myself available to you to fix the problem and put you back
on track."

I'm stunned by her revelation. I'm not sure where exactly
it's coming from, but I know I have to get to the bottom of it.

"I don't understand, Professor Richards..."

"Neve."

"OK, Neve. I know this stuff like the back of my hand.
There must be some type of mistake."

"Don't panic, Mandingo. I assure you that we can work
this out. Just meet me tomorrow in my office. I have some
research to get done so it'll have to be after 5:30. But whenever you arrive, you'll have my undivided attention."

"OK. I'll be there."

She walks away and many of the frowns on the faces of
the women turn to smiles. They feel satisfied that I've reject-

ed the white woman and decided to stick around and find someone to deal with of my own kind. But they're wrong. That's the furthest thing from my mind. I just want to be successful in America. I have to find out what's going on with Professor Richards' class. I have too many other problems to let my performance in school slip.

*****

I tossed and turned all night yet managed to make Denise think that everything was OK even though it wasn't.

It still isn't. My last class ended over two hours ago and I feel like a zombie watching all the students and professors leave for the night.

I still have a few moments before I can see Professor Richards so I concentrate on my surroundings. It's interesting to see the composition of the student body change from young kids who are just starting out and being nurtured by career educators to older students who are trying to pad their resumes to earn an extra couple of dollars an hour. Their helpers are adjunct professors, professionals out there in the workforce, gaining hands-on insight into the various industries they've mastered over the years. I just want to be the sponge that soaks up all the information.

When it's finally time to see Professor Richards, Neve, I feel a little uneasy. I hope it's not bad. I can't afford to let whatever problem I have go on so long that I can't salvage an A in the class. Getting all A's and one B is not an option for me. I have to achieve perfection. That's the only way anyone can make it in the real world when all the cards are stacked against them. All my people deal with the same type of deck.

*****

Neve is looking over some papers when I reach her office. She looks pretty calm so I start to feel a little better. Maybe my predicament isn't as miserable as I'm making myself think it is.

I knock lightly on the door and she looks up. She smiles when she sees that it's me.

"Come in, Mandingo," she says. "And please close the door behind yourself."

I close the door but she still gets up and locks it. She brushes against me both coming and going.

"You don't have to be nervous, Mandingo," she continues when she retakes her seat. "I know how important your grades are to you and I'm not trying to be a sore spot for you. I really do want to help you to make sure that you maintain your impressive performance here."

"I'm glad you feel that way because I do want to do well."

"And you're doing fine. You just need a few minor tweaks to get yourself back on track."

"Can you be a little more specific, Profess...Neve? I've been at my wits end since last night."

"OK. I'll try to explain it to you in a business sense and see if you can understand."

I give her my undivided attention.

"Imagine that you're fairly new in your position at a company and you're trying to get your feet wet. You do an OK job at learning and spend all of your time picking up whatever you can. Yet someone who started right around the time you did may not be putting in as many hours as you are but is seeing a little more success with the company. You can't figure out for the life of you why that is. Do you want me to tell you what's probably going on?"

"By all means." I'm confused.

"Well, while you're slaving and working, your peer is accepting every invitation for lunch, dinner, snack and after work drinks with the company brass. We like to call it schmoozing. So your co-worker may not be working as hard as you are at his actual job, but he is working hard at understanding that in business, one hand washes the other."

"So, you're saying that if you know which asses to kiss, it may be a little easier to get ahead to kiss them instead of killing yourself by working above and beyond what's expected of you. Oh, pardon my expression."

"Actually, that's alright. I'm actually quite happy you've used those particular words."

I raise an eyebrow to indicate that I'm still lost. She continues.

"If you know which asses to kiss in this country, you'll always be successful in this country, whether you're in business, or even if you're just a young college student trying to get an A. It's all about knowing what you have to give in order to get."

What was foggy to me starts clearing up.

"So, what is it that I have to give in order to get what I want and feel like I deserve?"

She sighs and slumps back in her chair. "I get so stressed out sometimes, Mandingo. I need something to take the edge off from time to time. Can you help me take the edge off?"

"How?" I ask even though I'm certain what she's referring to.

"I really liked that you used the term 'which asses to kiss'. I was hoping that we could start your extra credit program by your kissing mine."

"And that will help me to get an A?"

"It's already a done deal as far as I'm concerned."

"And like my co-worker, I don't have to work as hard at my actual job as long as I'm showing that I understand the way business works? The schmoozing part, I mean."

"You're learning, Mandingo. You're learning. But you do have to be here. Remember, appearances are everything. If you don't show up to class, how will anyone believe you can be successful in the real world?"

"I got you." I really do understand now what she's saying. "So what's next?"

She walks up to me and starts rubbing my chest. I'm not too turned on by how skinny she is but I do know that I have to give her what she wants in order to get what I want.

I try to just concentrate on her face without dissecting her body. She's cute but I can't trip too hard.

I look her in the eyes as she sucks on my dick and decide to give it to her whenever she feels like she's ready. Then I start imagining that I'm actually with Denise.

Sometimes you have to do whatever works.

In the end, I give her exactly what she needs and feel confident that I'll be maintaining my perfect average.

*****

When I get home, Denise is as supportive as always.

"How did everything work out, baby?"

"It's all good, now. Professor Richards helped me understand the part about business politics in this country that I wasn't getting. Now I'm back on track. I'm tired, though. I'm gonna take a shower and lay right down if you don't mind. It's been a long day."

It really has been a long day. Sometimes you just have to deal with being bamboozled and tricked into giving up some of the good dick when you have as much to work with as I do. By now, I've just gotten used to it.

CHAPTER TWENTY-THREE

Moriba

Spending so much time with Mariam has been really taxing on me. She's so loud and so annoying.

I'm glad that Fateema asked me to come over tonight.

I'm going to go out and buy myself some fresh digs, some of the clothes Fateema always tried to get me to wear but never would. I've decided to work hard to get totally back in her good graces and not just assume that I have her. I don't want to make the same mistake with her that I made with Kadija before I lost her.

*****

I arrive at my house in Harlem feeling like a new man. I'm so fresh and so clean just like Outkast used to rap about.

Fateema is sitting on the couch when I arrive. She looks as sexy as ever. I start to wonder if things would have been different if I would have just waited her out as far as having kids is concerned.

Fateema has really always been my pride and joy. I went to Kadija mostly because my feelings were hurt when she told me she wouldn't have my baby.

*****

Fateema is sitting on the couch as quiet as I am. I'm wrapped up in my thoughts but I wonder what her excuse is. I decide to break the ice.

"Fateema, I wanted to talk to you about something," I say.

"Me, too."

"Do you mind if I go first?"

"No. That'll give me some time to gather my thoughts."

"Is everything alright?"

"Yeah." She pauses. "You can go ahead. I'll be fine."

I gulp and swallow hard. I decide to go for broke. She's already my wife, so it's not like I have to beg her. But I really am trying not to make the same mistake twice.

"Fateema, I wanted to apologize to you for something that happened a long time ago. I mean, I hope I didn't put too much pressure on you before to have my baby. I should have let you get there in your own time."

She looks like she's seen a ghost.

"Why did you want to talk about this now, Moriba?"

"Because I feel like I'm losing you and I want to do better. I do still have a chance to work things out with you, don't I?"

She looks flustered.

"Moriba, you silly man."

"What do you mean?"

"You're always a day late with everything. A day late and a dollar short, as the Americans say."

"Can you just explain yourself?" I find myself starting to get frustrated.

"I can explain myself but I'm not sure you're gonna be too happy with me once I do."

"Well, try me."

"I can't. It's so hard to say."

I give her a mean, blank stare.

"Moriba, this really is difficult. I know I've been somewhat stand-offish with you at times but I do care about your feelings."

"Fateema, what the hell are you talking about?"

"Are you really gonna make me tell you?"

"Fateema, this is getting ridiculous."

"I know and I'm sorry but I feel so bad."

I've had enough so I grab her shoulders and start shaking her.

"Woman, just tell me what's going on."

I squeeze her shoulders harder. Her stalling is really starting to piss me off.

"OK but you have to let me go first, Moriba." I raise my eyebrows at her. "I mean it. Let go!"

I let her go and she moves a few inches away from me on the couch. Her strange behavior is really ticking me off.

"OK, Moriba. There's no other way to say it. I'm pregnant."

I immediately cheer up.

"That's wonderful."

"No, it's not wonderful, Moriba."

"OK, then. It's great if you don't want to call it wonderful."

"Moriba, it's not wonderful and it's not great. It's a catastrophe."

"Nonsense."

"It's..."

"I didn't hear you. Why are you mumbling?"

"Dammit, Moriba. I fucked up. It's Mandingo's baby, OK? So it's not wonderful."

I fall back onto the couch like I've just been hit by a brick.

"I'm sorry, baby, but I messed up. I never meant to hurt you like this."

I'm pissed as hell but I have a solution. "It'll be OK. You'll just get rid of it. But don't tell anyone outside the clinic. This has to be our secret."

"I don't think you understand, Moriba. I'm having this baby."

"No, you're not."

"Yes I am."

"Mandingo is my nephew. You're not having his baby."

"I am."

"Over my dead body you will! I promise you, it will never happen."

"I am, Moriba. I am."

"I promise you that you won't, Fateema. If you don't believe anything else, you can believe that."

I don't wait around for her to say another word. I get up and walk out, slamming the door behind me.

CHAPTER TWENTY-FOUR

Denise

Since Mandingo's been so stressed out by the police and school, I decide to treat him to dinner at one of his favorite restaurants, Bon Appetit on 112th. Yes, Mandingo has his own money now and has for a while, but it never hurts to be treated. Sometimes it reinforces the fact that a person cares about you.

As much as Mandingo loves the food here, I think he doesn't come much because the way the food is prepared reminds him too much of his homeland. I can always see the pain in his eyes.

I try to cheer him up by holding a pleasant conversation. I even joke about how his nice dick has everyone in the city at his mercy. He laughs a little but I really wish there was something I could do to make him feel better. I hate to see him sad.

He does cheer up somewhat when the food arrives, though. He's ordered rice with peanut sauce, and I'm having grilled fish with couscous. We both share an order of aloko, fried banana plantains.

We eat and Mandingo starts to cheer up. I'm glad I've decided to just be there for him. Sometimes, that's all it takes — knowing that you are not alone in the world.

As we're finishing our meal, my cell phone starts ringing off the hook. I don't answer it the first couple times since I'm enjoying Mandingo so much and I know that he needs to relax. But eventually, I answer it. I don't want Mandingo to think I'm trying to hide anything.

"Hello... oh, hi. What made you call out of the blue? Are you checking on us just to see how we are?...What?...Get the fuck out of here!" I drop the phone like it's a hot potato but pick it back up a few seconds later. "You're bullshitting me, right? That can't be true...Yeah. You're right. We'll definitely be careful. I didn't hear you...What?...No! You're serious?...Yes, I have. He's right here... Yes, I'm sure... No. He was with me all night. I'm positive... Yes, I'm positive. What's all this about? You're shitting me... No!...You're shitting me!"

I pull the phone away from my ear momentarily.

"This cannot be fucking happening."

I slam the phone once on the table before putting it back to my ear.

"Listen. We're at Bon Appetit. We're not going anywhere else. We'll just wait here for you. Get here as fast as you can."

I hang up the phone, feeling beyond worried.

"Who was that?" Mandingo asks. I'm sure he can see the worry on my face.

"That was Gineesmo."

"What the hell did he want?"

"It's terrible, Mandingo. Maybe I'll let him tell you. I can't bring you more pain."

"What do you mean, more pain? What the hell could have happened now? What more can there be?"

"There can be a lot more, Mandingo, a lot more."

I grab his hand and stroke it, refusing to say anything about what I've heard. He'll just have to hear it from Gineesmo.

CHAPTER TWENTY-FIVE

Mandingo

Gineesmo arrives not looking like his cocky, overconfident self, which happens to be a good look for him. He looks upset. It seems as if he's gritting on me like I'm about to make him lose his first case.

He doesn't waste any time. He doesn't even greet us. He just gets right to it when he joins us at our table.

"The mayor's wife, Denise? The police chief's wife? The fucking governor's wife? Is this a damn game to you, Denise? Who the fuck haven't you pissed off? Everybody who's anybody wants to see Mandingo go down."

"We don't ask for the husband's job description when the wife come to us. We don't always know who's buying our services."

"Turn to the fucking Metro section. Watch your local news. Do something. But don't act like you had no idea who some of these people were that you are now pissing off."

"Some of them but not all of them."

"A senator's wife...a judge...a congresswoman...a fucking transsexual."

"Transsexual?" Denise and I both say in unison.

"Oh, so you're telling me you didn't know about that one?"

"I hope you're bullshitting, Gineesmo." I turn to Denise. "What kind of screening process do you have?"

"Not a good enough one, apparently. But most of these people are very careful not to reveal their true identities. They come from influential families and have lots to lose if the skeletons in their closets fall out."

"This is making me sick," I say before turning to Gineesmo. "So, what else do you have to tell me? I mean, besides that everyone hates me."

"So, you still don't know?"

"I didn't tell him," Denise says. "I still don't believe it myself. Mandingo's been through too much pain. I didn't want to add onto it."

"Oh my God. We don't have much time. I may have been followed."

"What's going on, Gineesmo? What's going on, Denise?"

At that moment, what appears to be the entire New York City Police Department storms into the restaurant and surrounds me, weapons drawn.

"Don't make any sudden moves, Mandingo. Don't make any sudden moves."

"My client is innocent until proven guilty," Gineesmo says.

"Fuck you, Man," the cop that's putting the handcuffs on me says snidely. "Don't you have enough blood on your hands defending your other scum clients?"

"I only represent the innocent..."

"Bullshit!"

"That's why I win all my cases."

"Well, I don't know what kind of connections you may have had before but you've run out of miracles this time. Everyone wants to see this slime bag go down. Welcome to the realm of the losers, Gineesmo. How's it feel knowing you're about to fail for the first time in your career?"

"I only represent innocent clients, you little shit."

"Well, tell that to the judge. Your client will never get a jury trial."

With that, the cop walks me out the restaurant.

"Not to be a pain in the ass, sir," I say, "but last I checked, it's not a crime to sleep with someone. Why are you taking me away?"

"Good act, son," he says as he roughly shoves me into the back seat of the police car, banging my head on the door frame on purpose. He shuts me down then walks around to the passenger side and gets in. When his partner pulls away from the curb, he turns to me and says a mouthful.

"You are under the arrest for the murder of Fateema Nguse..."

"Aunt Fateema! You can't be serious."

"I'm dead serious. And don't interrupt me while I'm reading you your rights. Anything you say may be used against you in a court of law..."

"You have the wrong man. You know it's my uncle you should be questioning. It's always the husband."

"I don't know how you do things in Africa but your uncle

is not Fateema's husband. Now, you may have gotten away before but we have you hook, line and sinker this time. The autopsy shows that Fateema was pregnant with your baby. We already had your DNA on file so we just took the liberty…"

"Be quiet, Tom," the other officer chastises him. "We don't want to give Gineesmo any extra ammunition. Let's just seal his fate in court."

I start to wonder how I'm gonna get out of this mess. I'm not so sure that magic will be on my side this time.

CHAPTER TWENTY-SIX

Denise

Waiting for this trial has been so stressful, I don't know what to do with myself. The media has made such a frenzy out of it that I'm not sure if there's anywhere left in this country where Mandingo can go when he's found innocent. I can't help but feel like I've ruined his life. And that's exactly how Mandingo felt the last time I visited him just over a month ago. He's dead wrong, though. Dead wrong.

I'd found out the truth about Fateema and went to question him about it. Yes, I was upset when he confessed to having an affair with his aunt, but I didn't expect the conversation to go the way that it did.

I started by asking about the normal things you ask someone who's locked up. Are you OK? Are you getting enough to eat? Are the CO's treating you fairly? You know, things like that.

But eventually I had to get a couple things off of my chest. "Mandingo, I really need to know something," I said. "I have to know if you were honest about loving me or if you really were sleeping with your Aunt Fateema. And was she pregnant with your baby?"

"None of that matters," he answered. "The only thing that's important is that I need to get out of this place. I'm sad that Fateema's gone but I have to think about myself right now. I feel like I'm up shit creek without a paddle and I need a flotation device. I need all the support I can get. I don't need to be badgered right now."

"That's what you think? You think I'm badgering you? How am I supposed to feel when you act like I'm so important to you then run off with two of your aunts? And one of them ends up pregnant! We may never prove your uncle killed it but we know that you didn't. Still, you have to feel somewhat responsible for not controlling your hormones. Your uncle wouldn't have snapped like he did if you would have left his women alone."

"So, this is my fault, Denise?"

"You have to take a certain amount of responsibility for what you did to him — what you did to me."

"What did I do to you, Denise? And how in the hell did this get turned around to be about you in the first place?"

"You don't know?" I started crying. "I can't believe you don't realize what you've done to me and what you've done to us."

"Oh my God, Denise, I get it. I finally get it."

"Get what, Mandingo?'

"Guard!" he yelled.

"Get what, Mandingo? What are you talking about?" I pleaded.

"Guard! Guard!"

The guard came to take him away and left me alone with all my unanswered questions.

*****

Because Gineesmo and I are so close, I eventually find out that Mandingo thought I'd murdered both his aunts out of jealousy. He decided not to say anything so he could protect me, which seemed very admirable but was way off base. I couldn't kill anyone, yet alone someone in his family.

So for that reason more than any other, I got Gineesmo to hire the best private investigator he could find. I told him to spare no expense. I had to get to the bottom of it all.

In the end, Gineesmo learned some very interesting things. He won't tell me what they are, though. He says I just have to find out about them at the trial like everyone else.

I'll have to sit in the public area, though, if there's room since Mandingo doesn't want me in the area reserved for his loved ones. But regardless, I'll still be there for him. I have to be. That's what you do when you love someone the way I do him. You support them even when they tell you they don't want you to. You never give up on them. Never, no matter what.

CHAPTER TWENTY-SEVEN

Mandingo

As I am led into the courtroom for day one of my trial, I look around at all the high profile faces.

Damn. Gineesmo didn't lie.

As I scan the faces in the crowd, they look back at me. I see the mayor, the police chief, deputy police chiefs, several prominent businessmen. Everybody who is anybody is in the house and they all want to skin me alive. Gineesmo will have to do his finest work for me to have any chance of acquittal. I cross my fingers as the cuffs are removed, and I sit next to him. Then I close my eyes and rub them with my hands.

It's almost time to get this show on the road.

*****

The prosecution calls its first witness, the DNA expert. I'll soon find out if Gineesmo is as good as his reputation.

The expert confirms that Aunt Fateema was pregnant

when she was murdered and that the DNA report concludes that I am one hundred percent the man who impregnated her.

Gineesmo pops up out of his seat to cross examine the DNA expert. He doesn't waste a lot of time. He's very efficient in his questioning.

"Sir, you've testified that my client is definitely the father of Fateema's baby, given the DNA. Is that correct?"

"Yes, sir."

"Well, I just have one question. Is there any DNA evidence in your possession that proves beyond a shadow of a doubt that my client was with the deceased at the time of her murder?"

"Objection!"

"Your honor, the prosecutor opened up this line of questioning. Surely I have the opportunity to put on a defense?"

"Overruled."

"But your honor..." the prosector starts.

"Overruled," the judge interrupts and then turns to Gineesmo. "You're walking a fine line here, Counselor."

"Understood," Gineesmo replies. He turns back to the expert. "Please answer my question, sir. Do you have any physical evidence that proves beyond a shadow of a doubt that my client was with the deceased the night of the murder?"

"No, I don't."

"I didn't hear you, sir."

"No, I don't," he says louder.

"I have no more questions of this witness, your honor."

"Redirect?"

"Yes, sir," the prosecutor says. "Mr. Douowsky, can you

tell me your exact area of expertise?"

"Yes. I conduct analysis of blood, skin, and urine samples to determine the probability of a person's DNA involvement with a decedent."

"I didn't hear you say that you do any testing that confirms or denies the validity of a suspect's alibi."

"Because I don't."

"No further questions, your honor."

Gineesmo hops up.

"Mr. Douowsky, are you familiar with a case from 2003, State vs. Jefferson?"

"Objection!"

"Your honor. I'm counteracting direct testimony from Mr. Douowsky."

"I'll allow it."

"Mr. Douowsky?"

"I'm vaguely familiar with that case."

"Vaguely," Gineesmo says. "Are you sure that it's just vaguely?"

"Objection. The question has been asked and answered."

"I'll move on," Gineesmo says quickly. "I'll just refresh your memory. In State vs. Jefferson, the prosecution was able to determine that Mr. Jefferson did indeed know the decedent and refuted his claims that he'd never met her. Do you know how?"

Douowsky is silent.

"Do you know how, Mr. Douowsky?"

Douowsky's still silent.

"Your honor, please instruct Mr. Douowsky to answer the question."

"That's OK," Douowsky says. "DNA evidence."

"Do expound upon that please, sir."

"We found out that he knew the decedent by using DNA evidence."

"Your honor, I'd like permission to treat this person as a hostile witness."

"Objection."

"He won't answer my question, your honor."

The judge instructs Mr. Douowsky to answer the question.

"We found DNA evidence that proved that Mr. Jefferson was indeed in the home of the decedent. So he had to have known her."

"Is that all?"

"I'm not sure what you mean."

"Mr. Douowsky, is that all?"

"Mr. Jefferson was new to the neighborhood as he claimed. His alibi was that he hadn't yet arrived to New York City from Virginia, that he had been traveling during the time frame in which the decedent had to have been murdered. The fact that his DNA was found in the house shot down his alibi."

"So, DNA has been used to confirm or deny a person's alibi, unlike what you said earlier. Correct?"

"That's a different situation."

"Yes or no, Mr. Douowsky."

"Yes."

"I didn't hear you."

"Yes it has."

"I have no further questions of this witness, your honor."

*****

For two weeks, Gineesmo has been crushing the state's witnesses one by one during cross examination. What originally appeared to be an open and shut case was beginning to look like a joke. I anxiously await the judge so Gineesmo can put the finishing touches on my defense.

"All rise."

The judge is in chambers and I feel like I'm one step closer to being freed.

"You may be seated," the judge says. "Mr. Gineesmo, are you ready with your witnesses?"

"Your honor, I have only one witness. The defense calls Mrs. Chemise Goutier to the stand."

I'm totally baffled. I'm not sure what she has to do with this case.

"Can you state your name for the record?" Gineesmo asks once she's sworn in.

"I am Mrs. Chemise Goutier?"

"Can you state your name for the record?"

"Chemise Goutier."

"Can you state your name for the record, please?"

"Objection!" the DA yells. "Can we at least get past her name?"

"Before you sustain that, your honor, I'd like to explain why I can't seem to get past the witness's name. Please, may I have just a little latitude?"

"You have very little latitude, Mr. Gineesmo, and it's running out as we speak."

"Thank you, your honor." He turns back to Mrs. Goutier.

"I won't ask you to state your name for the record again. But I would like to know if you can tell me who Chemier Taylor Bey is?"

"Objection, your honor! What does this have to do with this case?" the prosecutor demands.

"Everything, your honor. It has everything to do with this case," Gineesmo shoots back.

"Overruled. You're running out of time, Mr. Gineesmo."

"OK. On the night of Fateema Nguse's murder, the surveillance camera at the A&P mini mart not two blocks from the scene of the murder very clearly shows you purchasing gasoline with a credit card. Can you explain that?"

"It's a coincidence, I guess."

"Alright. I'll move on. Can you explain why when we searched the A&P's records, there was no record of a credit card transaction made by a Chemise Goutier?"

"There must have been some mistake because I used one."

"Exactly. There was a mistake. But the mistake was yours."

"Objection! Is there a question anywhere in the horizon?"

"Mr. Gineesmo?"

"Can you explain to me why the surveillance camera shows you handing your credit card to the attendant at 21:13 hours and why the credit card receipt belonged to a Chemier Jackson Bey?"

"Objection, your honor! What does that have to do with this witness?"

"I'll allow it. I'd like to hear the answer myself."

"So, can you explain it?"

Mrs. Goutier is speechless.

"I'll ask another question, then. Can you tell me what type of practice Dr. Samuel Levins has in Norfolk, Virginia?"

"Your honor, please. Can we get back to the case?"

"Mr. Gineesmo..."

"Your honor. I'd like to submit into evidence defense exhibit one."

Gineesmo hands something to the court officer who in turn hands it to the judge. He looks at it and his eyes look like they're about to pop out of his head.

"Answer the question," the judge instructs Mrs. Goutier.

"He's a plastic surgeon." Tears start falling from Mrs. Goutier's eyes.

"And how do you know Dr. Levin?" Gineesmo continues.

She remains quiet.

"Your honor?"

"Answer the question."

"He was my plastic surgeon."

"So, did you have a nose job? A tummy tuck? Exactly what type of procedure did you have in Dr. Levins office?"

Mrs. Goutier is still quiet except for the slight sniffles that accompany the tears now freely flowing down her cheeks.

"Answer the question," the judge once again instructs.

"OK. OK." She finally breaks down. "You don't understand. No one understands."

"What don't we understand?" Gineesmo asks.

"I've had it so hard."

"It seems like you've had it pretty easy, lately. You're a long way from the projects in Virginia."

"Objection, your honor."

"Overruled."

"Your honor?"

"Overruled."

"I'm going to ask you one more time. What type of procedure did you have in Dr. Levins office?"

"I was born Chemier Jackson," she yells. "Are you happy now?"

There are many swoons throughout the courtroom so the judge bangs his gavel.

"I'll clear this courtroom if I have to. Quiet down."

"I only have two more questions, Chemier Jackson. What word is highlighted on both this copy of your birth certificate and surgical release form from Dr. Levins?"

"Male."

"Excuse me?"

"I said it says male. I was born a male."

The courtroom swoons again. The judge strikes his gavel and it quiets down.

"A black male?"

"Yes, a black male."

"But now you're a white woman."

"Yes."

I glance over at Mr. Goutier who appears to be sick. Come to think of it, I'm feeling kind of sick myself.

"I just have one more question, Mr. Jackson. Why? Why did you do it?"

He, she, or whatever is totally quiet.

"Your honor?"

"Be more specific, Mr. Gineesmo."

"Your credit card was used two blocks away from where the decedent was murdered. Not long before that, it was used near another of Mr. Moriba's acquaintance's place of residence the night she was murdered. You wanted to get caught, didn't you. So, why did you do it?"

By now, Mrs. Goutier and Mr. Jackson are both overwhelmed with tears.

"I wanted to set up Denise Jackson for killing his aunts. She took him away from me! Everyone hates Mandingo so much that all eyes fell on him and he was blamed. Look at him! He's so fine! I just had to have him for myself. Denise screwed it up then Kadija screwed it up. So I decided to make Denise take the blame for Kadija. Everything was fine until Fateema showed up wanting him and ended up pregnant. Everyone is trying to take him away from me! It's not fair!"

All of a sudden, Chemier jumps up wielding a decent size piece of wood he's somehow managed to rip off the witness chair and starts swinging it at the judge.

"Just let me out of here! Mandingo, I love you!" she/he yells.

The guard draws his weapon. "Back up, ma'am, sir. I will shoot you, I swear."

Before anyone knows what's happened. The officer cocks his pistol and shoots two bullets into Chemier Jackson's chest. The person I used to know as Mrs. Goutier drops to the floor, dead.

The courtroom is in an uproar. It takes twenty minutes for the judge to clear the courtroom and have everything return to normal.

"Mr. Prosecutor," says the judge, "do you have anything to add to this?"

"Your honor, in light of recent events, we'd like to drop all charges against the defendant."

"The court is in agreement. The defendant is free to go," the judge says, wrapping his gavel.

I stand up quickly and shake Gineesmo's hand. Then I rush out of the courtroom, promising myself that once I get out of dodge I'll never return to the United States again. It's better I just quit while I'm ahead. I definitely don't have any plans on pushing my luck.

CHAPTER TWENTY-EIGHT

Mandingo

I love New York City, but I won't miss it at all when we leave. It's been hard here for me. I guess that's why every inch of my body is telling me to just leave.

Our plane leaves first thing tomorrow morning, and Denise is taking me see a show at the Apollo Theater. I'm always talking about it.

I really love her. She always takes my wants and needs into consideration. She's not selfish like so many other women. Truthfully, she's a godsend, and I'm blessed to have her in my life.

Still, I will never let Denise live down the Chemise Goutier shit. Who'd ever have thought that Mrs. Goutier was born a man? I still spit ten times a day when I think about how many times I ate what I thought was her pussy.

But that confirms it. Looks can be deceiving. I'll never get caught up in looks alone again.

As much as I hated the situation, I really did have some

good times. I'll miss Mary Jane Beckam and miss my aunts. I'll even miss my uncle and plan to apologize to him someday.

Denise and I have decided to move to the Bahamas. I guess living there will be OK. It's warm and sunny all the time. We have lots of money so we'll be treated like royalty. And there will be plenty of beautiful women throwing themselves at us if Denise ever gets the urge to have a threesome again. I should just be happy. My life could be much worse.

****

Denise

I'm so nervous about leaving New York, but I'm happy I'll finally have Mandingo all to myself.

I had a good life, but I now realize that I hurt people. Psychologists are racking up in New York now because of my clients. Many freaked out when they found out that they had been sexually connected to a transsexual. I can't even imagine how Mr. Goutier feels.

I feel sorry for Mandingo, though, most of all. He is the manliest man I know. It must be tearing him apart, knowing what he did. And it can't help him to know that he was indirectly responsible for the murders of both his aunts and his unborn child. I hope he can be happy. That's all I ever wanted for him.

I was almost a millionaire before I met Mandingo. I'd worked years selling my body.

In the nine months I booked Mandingo, both officially and

unofficially, my share of his earnings are close to two million dollars. He's made both of us comfortable millionaires. Who would have thought that having a big dick could be so lucrative?

Truth be told, I'd give it all away if I could just be with him. He's all that's important in my life.

****

Mandingo

As I sit in my chair at the Apollo, I'm cheering and feeling happy. A young girl just finished singing Jennifer Holdiay's "And I'm Telling You I'm Not Going" to perfection. The entire theater is in an uproar.

I look around the room and a warm feeling enters my heart. It's feels good to be surrounded by so much love.

I look around me with a smile on my face until I see a white man who's not looking happy at all.

Why the fuck is he here if he's just gonna refuse to enjoy himself? I wonder.

I watch him walk around the theater, bumping into people, with that mean look on his face. Suddenly, the happiness I feel is gone.

I'm totally intrigued by him and his anger. My eyes are glued to him and so is my mind. The crowd is cheering, Denise is talking to me, but I don't hear her.

It's weird. I shouldn't be so focused on him, but a strange feeling comes over me. The man's not right.

He stops walking and throws open his coat to reveal a

semi-automatic weapon. Now I'm happy that I was concentrating on him. I have time to react.

As he lifts the weapon into the air and starts spraying the crowd with bullets, I push Denise to the floor and cover her body with mine.

I feel a sharp pain in my back but I'm not sure what it is. Before I know it, though, everything goes dark.

Then before I know it, it's bright again. So bright, in fact, that my eyes don't adjust right away and I have to blink several times.

When I can finally focus, I see that I'm no longer at the Apollo Theater in Harlem. I'm in the Bahamas with a group of hotties around me. I must be bugging because I'm not phased at all by any of them until…it can't be.

I see a sight for sore eyes. I don't know how it's happened but Denise has found me and rescues me from the lot of hoochies.

I run to her as fast as I can. She drops all of her bags and flies into my arms.

I kiss her as passionately as I can. At this point, I know I really love her. I'm stuck with her. I can finally be happy.

*****

It's after four and the sun is beating down on us. This is the busiest time of day. Yet I don't care about anyone else but Denise.

We rush to the beach and find an isolated spot on the sand, far away from the crowds. I peel off her clothes and she peels off mine and we make passionate love on the beach as if it was our first time ever. I don't care if anyone's watching. My life is finally complete. Even though I know I have a lot more time and much left to do, my life can end right now. I can't think of anything else to top this moment.

Finally, my life is complete. But truth be told, I'd go through everything all over again just to end up right here. With Denise is where I belong.

"Denise, oh, Denise."

"Oh, Mandingo, yes," she says in response. "Oh, Mandingo. Mandingo. Mandingo…"

*****

Denise

"Mandingo!" I yell, shaking him violently once the bullets have finally subsided. He isn't moving and he's barely breathing.

"Baby, please wake up," I beg. "I need you. I need you!"

My requests are falling on deaf ears. He can't hear me. No one can hear me.

It seems that the lifestyle we have led has finally caught up with us. His punishment is death and my punishment is living with the grief and guilt of knowing that I have everything to do it.

I grab him and hold him tightly in my arms. My man is gone and I pray to God that I die right now so I can be with him.

Living life is meaningless without him by my side.

Mandingo was a great man and now he's gone, I think.

Nothing will ever be the same.

EPILOGUE

Denise

Once again I wake up in the hospital, staring at a zombie. Mandingo has been in a coma for far too long. And the worst part of it all is that the doctors can't tell me whether or not he'll ever come out of it.

I think that karma is the realest thing on this earth. I knew it wasn't right to prod Mandingo to prostitute himself. We made so much damned money!

But I never looked at the bad effects it was having on the men and women who hired us. I only saw the green. Now I'm being served up a dose of my own medicine. And I can't stand the taste.

It's sad to say that I deserve this. I'm a nervous wreck not knowing what the end result will be. I'm hoping for a miracle, but know that I damned sure don't deserve one.

My life is over, just like Mandingo's. Shit.

Nothing else will ever be the same again.

Tamika
The Struggle of a Jamaican Girl

A new novel by
Sidi

A Novel

Tamika

The struggle of a Jamaican girl.

By **SIDI**

UTHOR OF FATOU, FATOU II AND THE LESBIAN'S WIFE

FORWARD

By an anonymous child molestation survivor

Dear Reader,
I am a victim of the same ordeal that's discussed in this story. I was very self-destructive before reaching the place in my life where I am today. I attempted suicide, chose negative environments, solicitied drugs and engaged in underage sexual behavior.

I had a baby at sixteen. But everything I did wasn't an outcome of that particular event in my life. Rather, the neglect and lack of communication between me and my mother led to my bad behavior.

When I used to look at myself in the mirror, I would think *Your life is not worth living so there's no need for you to exist.* So I used pills and knives to try to erase myself from the planet. But obviously they didn't work.

Then I began drinking and hanging with older crowds. I became an exotic dancer and started selling drugs. I didn't care about myself, and because older men liked my appearance and youth, I used both to my advantage.

I knew I wasn't getting over. I was just covering up for the things I felt inside. I convinced myself that I wasn't worth preserving, educating or even loving. So I ignored all my basic human needs and convinced myself that I was a waste of space.

I never disclosed this information verbally to my mother. But my actions were disrespectful, non-communicative and disconnected. When my mother finally noticed my behavior, she didn't ask me why. She just talked down to me in front of others. Eventually, our animosity turned physical and we fought. The result was that I ran away and got arrested.

I struggled every day with the fact that I was a teenage mom, not believing I was worthy of being someone's mother. My son loved me even if I didn't love myself. But I had sentenced my life to disaster before I even began to live it.

My mother would never have believed the attack that caused so much of my negative behavior. She put too much trust in her "man" and when I told her of his actions, she didn't believe me. That's what hurt me the most.

I didn't like my mother's boyfriend. She was so stuck on him—and the idea of having a man around—that she denied his abuse of me. And my disrespectful behavior towards her pretty much sealed the deal.

She didn't want to believe he could do wrong. He used to his advantage the fact that my mother and I weren't getting along and accused me of lying. She took his word over mine. Afterwards, I felt even more neglected, inferior and angry. And to add injury to insult, he stayed in my mother's life and I had to deal with him until the day came when she realized who he really was.

Don't think that every man or woman that enters your life is for the better. And don't think your child is up to no good simply because they may be going through an adolescent phase.

Investigate who bring around your children. It might prevent a lot of drama and pain.

My mother and I are getting along better now that I'm twenty-two but it took us a long time to get here. I love her but even my love increased the tension between us. We went into therapy together for a couple years. I still go alone twice a year to help me maintain the positive self image I finally achieved.

Now I help counsel teenage girls with my grandmother and have plans to become a hypnotherapist. Helping teens sort out some of the confusion in their lives is my goal.

My advice is to talk to your children as much as possible, even if they seem a little distant. So much can happen when you don't pay attention to them. Watch their behavior patterns. If they change drastically for the worse, something could be very wrong.

If through my experiences I can open eyes, draw attention to the relationship between parent and child, and help bring closure to their issues, I will be satisfied in knowing that I didn't suffer for no reason.

Sincerely,
Ms. Anonymous

PROLOGUE

"Cappy, no!" I screamed. I pushed and squirmed, but my little body was no match for the six foot five inch frame that was pinning me down.

"You'll get in a lot of trouble for this, Cappy! They aren't kind to ex-cops and pedophiles in prison. Cappy, nooooooooooooo!"

Tears streamed down my face. Snot leaked out of my nose. My breathing was very deliberate like I was about to have a panic attack. But none of that mattered to Cappy.

"Cappy, please. Noooooooooooooooooooo!" I screamed again.

I reached up and scratched his face as deeply as I could.

"You little bitch!" Cappy snapped as he backhanded me across my cheek. It felt like he was peeling my skin off.

"Lay the hell down and relax, you little whore! It'll be fun. Just chill. You'll be loving it by the time it's over."

Cappy leaned down and started nibbling on my ear and kissing on my neck.

"Besides, haven't I been good to you? Haven't I been taking good care of you since your dad's been gone?"

Save for my whimpering and sniffling, I didn't utter a sound. But Cappy wasn't moved. He continued his little speech as if he could break me down. But that was something he could never do.

"I deserve this little reward, Tamika. I deserve it."

With that, he forced his man-sized penis into my child-sized virginal walls. I felt pain, like I was being pricked by hundreds of hot safety pins after they were sterilized with a match.

But splinters weren't removed from my vagina that day, just my virginity. Blood splattered the sheets and my tears drenched the pillow. Between my blood and tears, I was probably dehydrated that day. But I was too young to know. I was too young to know.

The only other time I cried as much as I did then was the day I finally stopped Cappy's abuse. Yet I'm unsure why I cried. He didn't deserve a single tear.

That day, Cappy had come home and immediately started pitching a bitch about how dirty the house was. My mom had gone to the store to buy laundry detergent and the clothes she had been sorting were strewn all over the kitchen floor.

"Where's your mom?" he barked. I don't know why he thought I'd answer. I never spoke to him, ever, after he'd started abusing me.

"You are such a smart-ass little bitch! I work my ass off taking care of this household and this is the thanks I get?"

I rolled my eyes. Truth be told, even though my dad was arrested for being a kingpin, my mom got a thousand dollars a month from him. He set up an account just in case he ever got locked up. He wanted to make sure that there was enough money to take care of me until I turned nineteen.

"Then," Dad used to say jokingly, "You're on you own." Well,

I was already on my own even though I wasn't yet nineteen. I already had to be as smart as any adult.

When Cappy took off his gun belt and uniform and draped them across the chair, I set my expression to show him that I wasn't going to fight back that day.

"Why don't you let me get a little bit while I'm on my lunch? I always love a nooner."

I didn't comment.

"Let's go the bedroom, though," he said. "I don't want the neighbors getting nosy. They would never understand our love."

I almost puked, but I followed him up the stairs to my mother's bedroom anyway.

I followed him into the room and when he was completely naked, I backed away.

"I gotta pee," I said and slyly walked out the room.

"Fuck, Tamika!" he yelled after me. "Hurry up!"

Trust me. I am hurrying, I remember thinking.

That day, the upstairs toilet was not working well and Cappy knew I'd have to run downstairs and use the one near the kitchen instead.

I rushed past the bathroom and ran into the kitchen. I tried to be as quiet as possible but I was crying so hard that it was difficult to stop myself from sniffling. I didn't want Cappy to know I was crying.

I grabbed the gun from his belt, making sure to remove the safety. Then I headed back upstairs to my destiny.

This is one nigga who's gonna get what he deserves.

BOOK ONE

My Early Years

CHAPTER ONE

Upside Down

Age 9

I loved my dad. We did everything together. With his Kingston, Jamaican accent, ripped abs, bulging muscles, chocolate complexion, side-splitting sense of humor, and confidence, I just adored him. I wanted my future husband be just like him.

Yet as crazy as I was about my dad, my mom acted like she was twice as crazy about him. So much so that Dad often told her to stop acting jealous of me.

We went to basketball and football games, fishing, skating, bowling. We pretty much did some of everything.

And my dad was the only thug I'd ever heard of who took the time to figure out how to do his daughter's hair. Yes, he struggled through it every time, but he never sent me away when he got frustrated with my wet mop. He took pride in being there for me in every way, making sure my hair always looked pretty — braids, berets, everything.

It could have been embarrassing. But my adoration of him far surpassed any embarrassment I might have felt. I mean, what little girl shops with her dad for her first training bra? Well, I did. And he was as hands-on in the process as any mother would have been.

"Nah, Ma. Her nipples are still showing through material," he had snapped to the salesperson, "She's gonna need something a lot thicker to cover them up for real."

All I could do was put my head down and wish that I could crawl under a rock. He sounded so ghetto. It was embarrassing as hell. But he was there, and for that I was grateful. I felt so much better off than most of the girls in my neighborhood.

I can't tell you how many of the girls in my neighborhood grew up without fathers. They would skip town as soon as they found out they had gotten their women pregnant. They wanted no part of the responsibility. But my dad, he was down for me in every way possible. He'd always been my rock, for real.

Dad didn't know that I knew, but he was planning a big surprise party for my tenth birthday. He wanted me to celebrate it in style. Of course he didn't tell me about it. But come on now! He dragged me all over the place—linen stores, event planners, caterers. What business did my dad have in those places if something real serious wasn't about to go down?

The last place we went was the worst. Not because of where we were going but because of what happened when we were going there.

We were on the Brooklyn Queens Expressway, leaving Harlem and heading to a shop in Queens. All of a sudden, I saw flashing blue lights behind us.

When I turned around, there was a cop car behind us. My dad swore and pulled the car over.

"Don't worry, Tamika," he said. "All my shit is right so we won't get sweated too hard by these Jakes."

I immediately relaxed. Everything my dad told me was the law. So if Dad said it was OK, then it would be OK. Or so I thought.

"Can I see your license and registration?" said the officer that I later learned was named Cappy.

"I guess so," my dad said sarcastically. "But first, can you tell me why you stopped me? I'm going thirty-five in a thirty-five mile an hour zone, so I'm not speeding. It's light outside so you can't say a headlight's not working. I don't have any warrants…"

"Enough," Cappy spat out like he was large and in charge. "I'm the one asking the questions here. You don't need to be saying anything unless I ask you to."

"Whatever," my dad said, handing Cappy his documents. "Just make this fast. I'm taking my daughter somewhere, and we don't have all day."

"We'll see about that," Cappy said as he walked away.

We sat fidgeting in our seats without talking. I could tell that my dad was irked. That was the only time he didn't talk me to death or clown around with me.

The funny thing, though, now that I think about it, is that the cops were always stopping me and my dad for something. I guess there's something to that profiling thing everyone talks about. I guess they see a black male in a nice ride and assume he's up to something.

And yes, my dad was usually up to something. But the cops didn't know that. I think they just wanted to keep a black man down.

"Excuse me, sir, can you step out of the car?" Cappy asked

when he returned to us.

"Excuse me?" my dad snapped back, heated.

"It appears that this car has been reported stolen, sir. You're gonna have to come with me."

"Man, you're crazy out your goddamned mind! This is my fucking car, yo. What type of shit is you on?"

"Sir, we can do this the easy way or the hard way," Cappy said. "This vehicle is coming up as stolen so you're gonna have to come with me. If there's some misunderstanding, it will be dealt with downtown. But for now, you have to come with me."

"This is bullshit!" my dad barked. "I ain't going nowhere until I call my attorney."

"You can call him when we get downtown," Cappy snapped back.

My dad ignored him. He closed the window, picked up his phone and dialed.

"Hello. This is Marley St. Jacques. I need to speak to Mr. Luigi. It's an emergency. OK, I'll hold briefly but you have to hurry up. Some cop is standing outside my car right now."

Dad waited a second.

"Mr. Luigi, can you meet me at the police station? I haven't been arrested yet but this cop is tripping, saying I have to go with him. He's saying that my car is stolen. What's that? Oh, we're on the BQE just leaving Harlem. Just come to the precinct closest to here. If they take me somewhere else, I'll call you back."

My dad ended the call and handed me his cell phone.

"Hit redial and let Mr. Luigi's office know what's going on. I gotta deal with this bullshit."

After he finished instructing to me, he opened his door and started to get out.

"You're a fucking smart ass, aren't you?" Cappy said while grabbing my dad and placing handcuffs on him.

"What about my daughter?" my dad asked. "She's a child! I just can't leave her here."

"She'll come with us and if a relative can't come to the station, social services will take her until one does."

"My daughter ain't going to no fucking social services!" my dad snapped at Cappy before hollering back at me while being placed in the cop car. "Call your mom, too, Tamika, so she can pick you up. And don't worry about me. I'll be fine. This is some bullshit and trust me, Luigi's gonna deal with it."

After securing my dad, Cappy walked back to the car and addressed me.

"You have to get out the car, too, little girl. It's about to be towed. You're gonna ride in the car with my partner."

Almost on cue, a big, nasty, monstrous looking bear of a man with sergeant stripes on his shoulder appeared.

"Come on with me, Shorty," he said licking his lips.

I had no choice, so I went with him. I sat in his squad car and prayed that everything would be alright with my dad. Little did I know, though, that my whole world was about to be turned upside down.

CHAPTER TWO

Daddy's Gone

Age 10

It had been almost two weeks and my dad wasn't home yet. I was beyond worried.

My mom was rushing me to finish getting ready. She said we were going to my aunt's house, but I knew she was trying to play me. We were undoubtedly about to head to my surprise party.

"Tamika! I'm not gonna tell you again to hurry the hell up," my mom yelled. "We gotta get outta here."

"Yes, ma'am."

I tried to pick up the pace a little. I didn't want to go to my party without my dad.

Just as I was almost done tying my sneakers, I heard the doorbell ring.

"Tamika, get the door!" my mom yelled. "And I hope your ass is done when you go get it."

"I'm finished, mom," I said as I ran down the stairs. Maybe my dad was playing with me by ringing the bell. I was so excited. But nothing could have ruined my good mood more than who

I saw when I opened the door.

Cappy's black ass was standing there in plain clothes looking like Shabba Ranks after a bad accident.

What the hell does he want? I thought when I saw him. I almost closed the door in his face.

"Mom! That cop who locked Daddy up is at the door," I said as rudely as I possibly could. And then I did close the door.

"What the fuck now?" Mom said, irritated. I heard her high heels clopping down the stairs.

When she opened the door, Cappy started talking to her. I couldn't hear what they were saying because they were whispering. I snuck up closer to my mom so I could hear but she spun around and spoke to me in a way I never heard before.

"Girl, get the hell outta my face when I'm talking to somebody! I hate when your ass is all up in my business!"

I was shocked. I slowly retreated to the kitchen, praying that whatever Cappy wanted didn't take long. He was like a bad luck charm to me, like a dark black cloud hovering over me. With him around, nothing good would happen.

After a few minutes, I heard the door close and my mom came into the kitchen.

"Tamika, something just came up. You're gonna have to catch a cab to your aunt's house." She handed me twenty dollars. "You know how to flag down a gypsy cab, right?"

"Awe, Mom. I gotta catch a cab? I want to go with you!"

"Well you don't get everything you want, child! I told you something's come up."

"Dag! I can't stand him!"

"Child, what the hell are you talking about?"

"That cop. He shows up and I know something bad's gonna happen. He gets on my nerves."

"Child, just go to your aunt's and enjoy the rest of your birthday. You and me, we can go shopping later."

"Mom, please!"

"Don't get on *my* damned nerves! I have to do something." She grabbed me and gave me a hug and kiss. "Have a good time and try not to do anything that upsets your aunt. Lord knows she's bipolar."

"OK, Mom. I love you," I said as she walked away. "But I wish you were going with me," I mumbled under my breath.

When I opened the door at my Aunt Toni's on 158th and Amsterdam everyone yelled "Surprise!"

I pretended to be for their benefit but I was far from surprised. What did surprise me was how phat the apartment looked.

There had to have been at least two hundred balloons, and flowers were everywhere. There was a fountain with an ice statue of me. Who in the hood ever had an ice statue? That was my dad. Going all out for his baby and not even around to see the result.

I tried to be strong but eventually I started to cry.

"Awe," my cousins swooned.

"She's all shook up," my cousin Sabrina chimed in. "I would be crying too, girl, if my dad did all this for me. But I can barely get him to come get me for the weekend or give me five dollars to go skating."

"Yeah, her dad is good as hell to his daughter," Aunt Toni added. "No one would ever say that he doesn't love his daughter. But what's taking your mom so long to park the car?"

"She's not parking the car, Aunt Toni," I said unenthusiasti-cally. "She's not coming. She gave me twenty dollars for cab fare here and back."

"What?! What do you mean she's not coming?" she snapped, irritated. "She's your mother. She's required to come to your birthday party!"

"Well, she said something came up. I begged her but she said no. It must be something real important." I was getting annoyed at my aunt for making me defend my mother when I was so angry at her myself. "You know how my mom gets when her mind's made up about something."

"Umm, umm, umm. Katrina gets on my damned nerves," Aunt Toni said. "Ain't nothing in the world gonna come up that would stop me from celebrating my daughter's birthday with her. And your dad's locked up for some bullshit and she knows you're upset about it. Sometimes I can't stand her fucking ass."

"Mom, can we just try to have fun?" my cousin Sabrina asked. I think she could tell that I was upset enough without her mother making me feel worse.

"Don't tell me what to do girl! I'm the parent."

That's how it was in my family. Children were seen and not heard, and we were often brushed off. And the adults always made shit about themselves. It was my birthday, my dad was in jail, my mom was who knows where, and my day was ruined. I started to wonder how my young life had turned so bad so fast. Living without my dad for two weeks was like living in hell.

We continued on with my so-called birthday party, but there was nothing happy about it. My aunt tried to cheer me up by allowing me to open my presents, but it didn't work.

I got clothes, and my aunt gave me a pair of earrings. But the best presents would have been to have my mom & dad there. The two people I loved and adored were not around for my 10th birthday.

My aunt was really pissed.

"Your mother is such a bitch for leaving you high and dry on your birthday. She's probably somewhere sucking some dick. I hate that selfish bitch."

That did not make me feel better. My mom was not a selfish bitch to me.

Then to make matters worse, the gift from my dad was a cheesy radio. I knew my dad would never have bought it for me. My mom probably picked it out and put his name on it. I may have been young but I was smart and savvy enough to know that my dad would never buy me such a thing.

"Don't you wanna cut your cake, honey?" my aunt asked. "It's your favorite".

I always loved strawberry shortcake. But that day, I didn't feel like eating any.

After the cake was cut and all the gifts were opened, I called my mom, hoping that she was on her way to get me. I called again and again but she didn't answer the phone. I fell asleep on my aunt's couch.

I woke up to an argument. Aunt Toni and my mom were going at it.

"Katrina, why were you out with that fucking man when your man is in jail?" my aunt asked.

"Keep your voice down, bitch. Can't you see my child is sleeping?" my mom said. "I gotta do what the fuck I gotta do."

Do what she has to do. I had no clue what they were arguing about but my virgin ears continued to take heed.

"You know, Cappy said he may be able to help Marley get out of jail if I help him out a little."

"What you mean 'help him out'?" my aunt asked.

Silence filled the room.

"I know you ain't fucking with that herb-ass pig," my aunt said. "That pussy ain't gonna help get Marley out and you know it."

"I ain't fuck him. I just spent some time with him and kicked some bullshit on him so he'll help me out," my mom said.

"Yeah, right. I know you better then that, girl. You better watch your back."

I began to cry. Even though I did not fully understand, I knew something was happening with that cop and my mom.

When my mom came to get me, I pretended to be fast asleep. I had buried my face in the cushions to wipe my tears so she wouldn't know I had been crying. She woke me up and led me to the car. She and my aunt did not exchange goodbyes. In fact, after that night, I don't remember them speaking much on the phone or in person.

We arrived home to a sight that I would never have believed if it wasn't happening right in front of me. Cappy was standing in front of our house, not wearing his uniform, not sitting in a cop car.

I mumbled, "What the fuck is he doing here?"

My mom balled her fist and punched my underdeveloped chest with all her might.

"Keep your grown-ass mouth closed! This man is going to help daddy get out of jail."

"You do what he says, 'Mika, whatever he says. Do you hear

me?"

I did not answer because she had knocked the wind out of me with the punch. When I looked up there was midnight looking in my window, reaching to open the door.

"Come on, sweetie. Let's go inside. Your mom says you've had a long day."

Who the fuck was he to call me sweetie and why was my mom telling this asshole who got my daddy locked up anything about me? And why was he at our house?

I paused but my mom nudged me so I had to get out of the car with his assistance.

"Tamika, Cappy is here because he felt so bad about what happened to your dad that he is trying to help us," my mom said.

"Help? We don't need his help," I blurted out as we entered the house.

"You need to control your child. Or should I put her in hand-cuffs?" Cappy said in a mean yet seductive way.

"I'll handle her, Cappy. You know how kids are these days."

She walked me to my room and told me to get my ass to bed fast or she would hit me again. I laid in bed wondering what had gotten into my mother and what my dad was thinking about at that moment. I prayed that he would come home soon and fix everything.

As I dreamt about my dad coming home, I felt a presence. I slowly opened my eyes. I got scared when I saw the whites of Cappy's eyes beaming down on me. Before I could scream, he covered my mouth.

"Listen, little girl. I'm in control now. You and your mom need me. I advise you to be nice to me or you will never see your dad again. His future is in my hands."

I could barely breathe. His beastly hands were smothering my nose & mouth. As my little body tried to maneuver out of his tight grip, I saw a shadow in the hallway.

Cappy quickly released me and turned all nice. "Good night, sweetie. Sleep tight."

I hated that word. Sweetie. I cried myself to sleep that night. I could not have imagined that Cappy would be the beginning of the end for me.

I prayed my daddy would come get me soon. I knew it was just a matter of time. So until then, I would obey my mom and say my prayers. Then the nightmare would be over.

I guess not all dreams come true.

My dad had been locked up for almost eight months. In the beginning, we visited him often, and my mom would tell me "Daddy will be home soon."

After a while, though, we stopped going to see him, and we saw Cappy more and more often.

I didn't tell my mom about Cappy's mysterious birthday message. I just sucked it up and tried to be as nice as possible. I wanted my daddy to come home. I needed my daddy to come home.

The long distance phone service had been cut off so my dad could not call me collect anymore. Mom and I were not doing good at all. We went from eating steak dinners to Oodles of Noodles. Sometimes three times a day. I remember my mom cried a lot about needing my dad and that God needed to get her out of this mess. She didn't talk to me much. I felt like she blamed me for daddy being away.

Cappy continued to come over. At first he would nap on the couch. But before long, he was staying the night. The next thing I knew, he was in bed with my mom.

One night I could not sleep, and it dawned on my young soul what was going on.

I had gotten up to use the bathroom, and as I walked past my mom's closed bedroom door, I heard her crying.

"Cappy, I can't do this anymore," I heard her say. "I love Marley. But he ain't never coming home, is he?" She was crying hysterically.

"Shut the fuck up, bitch! That nigga don't love you. He lied to you about everything. That's why he's still locked up. I can't help it that he is where he is. He better not drop the soap."

I hated Cappy. I wanted to go in there and kill him. My dad was my life. Why was my mom crying in front of that nigga like he was the truth? My dad was the man, in or out of jail. He did everything for us. Cappy didn't do shit for us.

I remember hearing Cappy laughing.

"You's a dumb bitch! Marley ain't comin' home no time soon. Now, after I fucked you and knocked you up, you gotta stay with me. You think Marley gon' take care of another man's baby even if he does come home?"

My mom started screaming then. "I hate you! I hate you! I ain't having this bastard baby! NEVER!!"

I thought to myself, BABY? I'm her BABY. What the hell was going on?

I huddled on the bathroom floor, which would become a common thing for me to do, and wondered what I should do next. I was only ten years old and had no clue about all that adult bullshit. All I wanted was for my daddy to come home and make my life perfect again.

I started to go back to my bedroom but I heard all this cussin' and screamin' so I opened my mom's door. Cappy had her on the floor, but I couldn't tell what was going on.

"You know you love this dick inside of you girl. Marley can't fuck you like this. That's why I'm here and he's not."

"Please stop, Cappy! My daughter might wake up."

"She old enough to know what dick is!" he shouted.

I did not know then. But I learned in the next minute.

What Cappy was doing to my mom was the nastiest thing I had ever seen. I always had turned my head on the kissing parts in the movies. But it was my mom so I watched. It didn't look like she was enjoying what Cappy was doing to her.

"I'm gonna fuck you til you can't fuck no more."

"Cappy, I'm pregnant with your child! Have some respect!"

"I'll stop if you tell me you love me."

"Cappy, I love Marley," my mom cried.

A sigh of relief came over me. I could not understand why she was with Cappy in the first place. I wanted to go in the room and stop him but I was scared, so scared. I knew I would get into so much trouble. Maybe that's how grown people have fun, I reasoned. I had no clue.

After about ten minutes, I went back to the bathroom and flushed the toilet, hoping they would stop. I was wrong. It seemed like my mom's screams got louder and louder.

"Mom," I yelled. "MOM!" I yelled even louder.

"Yes, baby?"

"Are you OK?"

"Yes, baby. Go back to bed."

As I proceeded to my room, Cappy came out butt naked with

a hard dick and sweat dripping down his face.

"Excuse me, Tamika. I thought you were in bed. That's usually where little girls are at this time of night," he said with an ugly look on his face.

I ran to my room, locked the door and jumped under the covers. I was scared to death. All I could think about was my daddy and how he was so protective of me. I knew that if he knew what was going on, he would have killed Cappy.

Twenty minutes later, I heard a knock on the door.

"'Mika, baby, it's me. Open the door," my mom said in a low whisper.

I jumped up to open the door.

"Mom! Are you OK?" I hugged her tight.

"Yes, baby. I'm fine. We were just playing."

I knew she was lying. I could see the tracks of dried tears on her cheeks.

"Mom, when is daddy coming home?"

"Soon, baby. Very soon. I hope."

"Mommy, why is Cappy here? He got daddy locked up, and he's not treating us right."

"Baby, just a little while longer and we won't have to worry about him at all."

I had never seen my mom look so lost and alone. My dad was always there to help her. Now she seemed so helpless and desperate even to my young eyes. She kissed me on my head and told me to get some rest. I never even thought to ask if I was having a baby sister.

The next morning, I woke up to paramedics in my living room. My mom was on the couch and Cappy was holding her hand.

"Mommy, what's wrong?" I rushed to her.

"Everything is OK, 'Mika. Mommy just has to go to the hospital for a little while, OK?"

"Why?" I cried.

That's when Cappy came over to "rescue" me. But all I wanted him to do was die. I hated him and was embarrassed, especially because I saw his long black dick.

"Your mom is going to be OK, 'Mika. Just calm down."

My mom was taken by ambulance to the hospital. I stayed home by myself because Cappy said I was too young to know what was going on.

It was bullshit. I knew that whatever he had done to my mom had hurt her and hurt her bad. My mom hated hospitals. She didn't even go to see her favorite uncle when he was in the hospital dying from AIDS.

She must have really been sick. I cried until I couldn't cry anymore. I had no one to protect anymore and I had no one to protect me anymore. I started to believe that my daddy didn't care. If he loved me, then why didn't he break out of jail and come and save our family?

Later that night while I was asleep on the couch, I jumped when I heard the front door crack open. I cried, "Mommy!" but I soon realized it was not my mom. It was that black creature sent from hell.

"Shut up, girl. Your mom will be here in the morning. We'll go together to pick her up. Go back to sleep."

"Cappy, what's wrong with my mom?"

"She was having my baby and it died because your dad put a curse on it from jail. You see, Tamika, sweetie, me and your mom are together as man and woman. You know, boyfriend and girl-friend?"

I looked at him all confused. My mom and dad would never be apart. What was he talking about?

"Your dad doesn't want you anymore. That's why he hasn't called. He has no interest in you or your mom. So now I am going to be your dad. I'll take care of you, don't you worry."

"My daddy will be home soon. My mommy's only being nice to you so you can help him get out."

"Little girl, you have no clue about life. Your mom is a slut and you will be one too if a real man not a drug dealer like your dad doesn't step in and mold you to be what you are supposed to be. Go to bed, little girl."

"When my dad gets home, he's gonna fuck you up for being mean to me. I am his princess and my mom is his queen and you are just a piece of shit!"

As soon as the words left my mouth, I realized that I had gone too far.

Cappy came close to me and snarled in my ear, "GO TO BED, little girl, before I fuck you up."

I ran up the stairs and tried to lock my door but the lock was broken.

Oh no! What now? Think, Tamika. Think!

I ran and hid under my covers. I was crying and praying for my parents to come home.

After a while, I feel asleep. I felt a presence again but I did not move. I just laid still, hoping he would go away. He didn't.

I felt cool air on my legs as he lifted up the corner of my quilt. Then Cappy's big, black hand reached in my Sunday panties to touch my "pocketbook" as me and Mom called it.

My dad always told me not to let anybody go into my pocketbook, especially a man.

I really didn't understand what he was talking about at the time. But then all of a sudden I did.

Cappy's huge fingers slipped inside my pocketbook. He hurt me so bad but I was too scared to scream. I was mad at myself for not obeying my dad. And even if I had screamed, who would've heard me?

My mom was gone and my dad was in jail. It was just me and the beast.

As he touched what I would soon learn was my pussy, I heard him say, "Oh my God. This feels so good. I want this tight pussy."

I tried to peek out from under the covers to see what he was doing. All I could see was one hand in his pants and feel the other in mine. It was awful.

I knew he knew I was awake because I began to cry. But the louder I got, the more he seemed to enjoy it.

He pressed his fingers harder and harder inside of me until I heard and felt something rip.

I was burning. I pleaded with him, "Stop, Cappy! I want my daddy."

"Fuck your daddy! It's time for you to become a woman."

A woman? I was ten years old!

As I laid there being brutally molested by a grown-ass man, I began to say the Lord's prayer. "Our father, who art in heaven, hallowed be thy name…"

The next thing I heard was Cappy groaning loudly over my

whisper.

"Oh shit! Oh shit! I'm comin'! I'm fuckin' comin'! AHHH-HHH! Damn!"

I didn't know where he was going but I was glad it was over. He pulled his hand out of me and left.

I laid there quietly crying to myself. I wondered how and why my life had become so messed up so fast. Had I been a bad little girl like my mother said I was sometimes? Did I deserve everything that was happening? Was I the cause of my family being in ruins?

As I laid there thinking, the beast came back in the room.

"Sweetie clean up," he ordered. "I think you're bleeding. You probably got your period."

I got up without a word and went into my dresser drawer and took out the pad from the packet we got in health class three months prior when we were taught about the birds and the bees.

I washed off, put the pad inside a fresh pair of panties, and got back into bed. I avoided the spreading blood stain on my sheets.

I knew then for certain that Cappy was truly the devil. I didn't understand before what a nasty motherfucker he was. He had fondled and molested my young pussy and didn't care about the blood or anything.

I was so ashamed. I didn't know what to do. I was too young to know what had happened to me. All I knew was that I was alone in the house with that black devil and it didn't feel good.

I felt the same way my mommy had looked the night before, bruised and hurt.

I started to wonder about what Cappy had said. Did my

daddy not want me anymore? Maybe it was true. All I could do was think and cry and pray that if I was good, things would get better.

Also by

Sidi...

FATOU

AN AFRICAN GIRL IN HARLEM

By Sidi

A Novel

Fatou
An African Girl in Harlem

Twelve year old Fatou travels from West Africa to America thinking she's furthering her education. Yet, she arrives in New york City greeted by a man three times her age—someone from her village who paid a dowry to be her husband. Suffering through pedophiles, deplorably cruel living conditions, and a slave-life job eventually pushes her over the edge. When the smoke clears, she refuses to be a victim and exerts control of her life by becoming part of Harlem's fast money scene. The resulting terror leveled at anyone who gets in her way doesn't mask her old wounds but it does soothe her overwhelming hunger for revenge. Aside from money,power,respect,and her new love for New York city's number one drug lord, that's all a West African girl in Harlem has to look forward to.

This fast paced novel examines what happens when the bonds of family and tradition fall apart. And it shows how a strong and fearless woman can hold her own surrounded by grimey men in the dangerous drug game.

FATOU

Return To Harlem
Part 2

By Sidi

A Novel

Fatou Part 2
Return to Harlem

With the love of her life mysteriously murdered, West African Harlemite Fatou sets out to discover- which of her murdered lover's lieutenants in New York City's most notorious drug cartel was responsible for setting him up. After finally getting to a peaceful state in her own life despite suffering through pedophilia, rape, being kidnapped, and working under slave labor type wages, the death of the man that picked her up when she was down finally pushes Fatou over the edge. And, although the lieutenants mistakenly assume that the death of Fatou's lover will soften the reigns of her control, they find out that he was the one that had previously cooled her down when she was about to blast off. There will be no such luck now that Fatou is on her own and poised to exact revenge. Everyone around her will find out what happens when a woman with an attitude is in control and determined to get respect one beat down at a time.

The rage in this story of revenge is furious and shows you that you'd be better off antagonizing a ravenous pit-bull than to get on the wrong side of the wrong woman. Beware everyone because Fatou is back with a vengeance. I advise everyone to duck, put down your shades, and close your curtains. Don't be caught in the path of her wrath.

*And read an excerpt
of the latest novel by*

Sidi…

The Lesbian's Wife

A Novel By

SIDI

PROLOGUE

I'm staring at Sharyn in disbelief, not knowing why she wants me to rehash every horrific detail regarding my life over the past four years. The pain that I endured makes me want to scratch someone's eyeballs out. And since Sharyn is the person responsible for my tears right now, I'm thinking that it might be hers.

"It's best if you just let it out, Aisha," she says.

"No, it's Nikki. Don't ever call me Aisha again. I mean it, Sharyn! Don't ever call me Aisha."

My entire body is shaking and tears are streaming down both my cheeks and neck. I'm furious at Sharyn for taking me back to a place I never want to go again. But I can't be too mad at her, though. If it weren't for her, I'd still be captive. My life would still be a living hell.

Maybe I shouldn't have gone through life half asleep. Maybe if I would've paid attention to what was going on around me, I wouldn't have ended up a victim. Maybe I could have done something differently. I say that, but I know that there really wasn't anything that could've been done differently, and if Sharyn hasn't done anything else, she's convinced me that I am not to blame for the tragedy I suffered at the hands of a crazy man.

"He's the one who was wrong, Nikki," Sharyn says right on cue. "He's the monster, and you were the innocent victim."

Fuck that, I think to myself.

I hate the fact that I was a victim. I know that I never wanted to be. Yet, as much as I want to say that I'll never be a victim again, I just can't say it. In life there are no guarantees. I'd loved to say that I'd die before I'd be a victim again. But when I was a victim, I was too afraid to put myself out of my misery. To the contrary, I endured every little bit of the torture. And that's what scares me the most, knowing that I didn't take extreme measures to end my suffering, and if I ever again had to face a nightmare like the one I just escaped, I don't know if I could.

I rarely sleep through the night anymore. I always wake up shaking, sweating and terrified. I'm convinced that I'm on Africa's Ivory Coast instead of being safe and sound in America.

The funny thing is that I was so in a hurry to go to Africa. Who wouldn't be? Africa is the cradle of all civilization. I'd advise everyone to visit the motherland at least once in their lifetime if they have the chance. Well, at least I would have advised them of such in the past, but now I'm not so sure. I think if it's a woman, I'd tell her that she'd better be careful. I wouldn't want what happened to me to happen to her. I don't think I'd wish that on my worse enemy.

If a woman doesn't have a pack of girlfriends to go with her, I'd tell her to travel as much as she wants as long as it's in America. There are hunters out there in foreign countries, and believe it or not, young, attractive women are the prey. And if you're foreign to that country, you have very few resources to depend on for help. You're pretty much out on your own and forced to depend on yourself for survival. Some make it and some don't. And psychologically, some overcome the tragedy and some don't. The cruelties they suffered at the hands of the abusive male scum of the earth defines the rest of their lives and they're unable to function. They're lost within their abduction and no one knows if they'll ever be found.

That's why I really do hope that all women take me seriously. Yes, I'm trying to get my own head together, but when I do, I plan to speak to women about the perils they will face out there in foreign lands. And if I save one life—if I prevent one woman from going through what I went through—all the tears that I'll shed while rehashing my own horrible story will be worth it.

Take heed of my story. Pay very close attention to the mistakes I made. No, pay close attention to everything I did, especially the things that any normal young girl would have done. Because you never know who's going to sell you down the river. You never know who's going to turn his back on you and put you in a position where you're lost and lonely in a foreign land with no one to turn to. All you'll know is that you're abducted and at the whim of whomever stole you away.

So listen up ladies because it could be you. It could happen to you.

BOOK ONE

Warning Signs

CHAPTER ONE

Atheist

How I was able to grow up an atheist in an Islamic home in New York City, the pinnacle of Islam in America, I'll never know. How I was able to hide my atheism from my father, an African immigrant who became a naturalized American citizen and who also eventually became the most respected African in New York City, I'll never know. But I do know when I became an atheist. In fact, I remember it like it was yesterday. I'll never forget what happened that day.

I was coming home from school, excited to tell my mother about my audition with and acceptance into New York City's prestigious Performing Arts High School.

I heard the commotion from about a block away. Of course I knew where it was coming from because this wasn't the first time my house was the center of attention on the block. There was always some type of domestic disturbance happening there. Yet I ran as fast as I could anyway, hoping that my presence would make a difference.

As I approached my house, I slowed down. I could hear men making snide remarks about how my mother must have acted up again. Of course all the men I'm referring were wearing Muslim garb. They never mattered to me—not then, not now. Yet, I do remember thinking that they had nerve. My mother was a grown woman so I couldn't fathom what they meant by saying that she was acting up again. But as bad as those bastards were, they were nothing compared to the men inside my house.

There were maybe five Muslim brothers yelling at my mother as she cowered in the corner, blood dripping from her nose and mouth.

"What were you thinking, Aminata? A woman must honor her king. You've disrespected a great man—a great man! How could you question him? How could you have a dispute with his other wife? And then you get arrested and bring more shame upon his name?"

My mother cringed as my father stood in front of her and smacked her with the back of his hand with so much force that her head snapped back and banged into the wall. She collapsed on the floor.

But that didn't stop the gang of male Muslims from berating my mother further and telling her that her ass whipping was her own fault. They didn't even have mercy when my father kicked my mother so hard in her belly that she spit up blood. The beaten and defeated woman who I called Mom was chastised into submission as I watched in horror. All I can say now is that I was thankful that none of my younger sisters were there to witness what I witnessed.

As disturbing as the abuse of my mother was, what disturbed me even more was the attitude of the Islamic males in the room that day. When the beating ended, they offered the following words of encouragement.

"Don't worry, Aminata. Allah will forgive you for your wayward acts if you ask him to. He is the most beneficent and merciful."

I remember thinking, *Mother fuck Allah and mother fuck you.* From that day forward, my heart never gave a damn about religion. And as if that day wasn't enough to make me hate religion, my father gave me plenty more examples of why his religion— or any religion for that matter—was for the birds. I was not going to kneel down just to give men an excuse to treat me like I wasn't shit, which is exactly how my father treated my mother.

I learned that my mother was beaten for speaking up about Mariama, the woman who claimed to be my father's third wife. In Islam, no woman is to question a man. So, in all honestly, I guess my mom should have known better. That was the life she'd been living for so long.

About a week before the beating, my mother was giving my father a bath and discovered scratches on his back and a passion mark on the right side of his neck. As silly as it sounds, my mother was upset because the passion mark wasn't on the left side of his neck. What bullshit. I get angry just thinking about it.

She and my father's second wife, Kadia, had made a pact that Kadia would suck on the left side of my father's neck and my mom would suck on the right side. So, of course, when Mom saw the mark on Dad's right side, she freaked out. She called Kadia the next day, and they got into a heated argument. I heard that they ended up fighting in the middle of Central Park and getting arrested for disorderly conduct.

They spent the night in jail and weren't able to get in touch with my father because he was out of town. Yet they did call the mosque and speak to one of the brothers who said that everything would be taken care of.

Well, a week before my father tried to kill my mother, I came home and saw Kadia and a woman I'd never seen before arguing in front of our house. It turned out that the woman had bailed them out of jail. Whoever they talked to at the mosque called my father and he must have instructed the woman to bail them out.

As any woman with an inquiring mind would have done, both my mother and Kadia asked the woman who she was and why she bailed them out. She told them that she bailed them out because that's what my father told her to do. They asked how she knew my father. She proceeded to whip up her finger in brag-gadocio and showed off a two carat diamond ring. Then she told them that she was my father's wife.

This next part of the story gives me a headache.

They all started to argue. "You're not his wife! I'm his wife!" But before it was over, my mother told Mariama that she could only suck on my father's chest because she had the right side of his neck and Kadia had the left. That's what they were arguing about when I showed up, even though I didn't know it at the time.

Excuse my French, but don't they sound like three dumb-ass bitches? I love my mother to death, but come on now! At some point you have to use your damned brain. I think that if she would have used her brain like my father used his dick, she would have been dangerous. Or maybe she was dangerous. What brain could come up with sick shit like you suck on one side of his neck, I suck on the other, and the odd woman out sucks on his chest? Yeah, my mom was dangerous.

Anyway, my father returned from out of town and warmed himself up on Kadia and Mariama for getting into his business prior to coming home to whip my mother's ass. The funny thing is, though, that even though she had advance warning of what was going to happen to her, she felt that because she was his first wife, she had rights.

So, to recap, my mother argued with the two bitches who were sleeping with my father, one of them called to tell her that my father had blackened her eye and fractured the other woman's arm, and my mother naively believed that she wouldn't get any of his treatment because she married him first. As far as America is concerned, my mother is considered to be my father's one true wife. And I'm the one who's supposedly screwed up because I'm an atheist? Yeah, OK.

As much as I hate Islam, and as much as I hate the grown-ass men who didn't protect my mother the day of her ass-whipping, and as much as I hate my father for the way that he treated my mother under the slick-ass disguise of Islam, I'm not trying to single out Muslims. My hate and disgust transcends all religions.

My best friend, Beyonce, is the daughter of a Baptist minister who also happens to be the pastor of a huge church in Manhattan. Beyonce's father isn't Muslim, but he's still a humdinger.

Beyonce told me about how her father used to molest her and her older sister once they reached puberty. What makes it so bad, though, is that Beyonce's mother is gorgeous. She has long, exotic, silky hair with so much life. I wish my hair was as manageable. But that's not all. She has the sexiest hazel green eyes. They would stop any man in his tracks. Add to that a nice plump ass, thick thighs, and no waist, and that's Beyonce's mother. Still in all, her father found the need to defile his own daughters.

Beyonce says that when she turned twelve or thirteen and moved from her training bra to a 34B, her father started to look at her funny. She says he made her feel crazy uncomfortable. But he's her father, right? So of course she thought she was tripping.

Well, one day when her mother was out shopping and her father had given her older sister money to go to the movies, Beyonce heard the bathroom door open while she was in the shower. Before she knew it, her father pulled the shower curtain open and looked at her the same way he'd been looking at her before. The rest is history.

Beyonce told her mother, but her mother didn't believe her. Then she tried to tell her older sister but her older sister burst out crying. At that point, Beyonce knew that she wasn't her father's first victim. So she just kept her mouth shut from then on and endured his molestation until she ran away at the age of sixteen. She's been on her own every since.

Beyonce keeps in touch with her family, though. That's how she found out about the bastard children her father has on Long Island and in the Bronx. I think there's three of them. Add to that five abortions that women who fucked him got, you can figure out that her father was definitely a rolling stone. But the worst part is that all the women with whom he had relations were members of his church. They all smiled in Beyonce's mother's face while sleeping with her man.

If it was me, I would have grabbed a gat, run into the church and went postal on all those bitches. But again, that would have been a woman doing something to another woman who's just as much the victim as she is.

Speaking of victims, Beyonce's mother ended up the biggest victim of them all. Her husband gave her HIV. She had a nervous breakdown and has never been the same.

Once again, a religious man of scriptures and passages ruined a woman's life. So I say to hell with religion. Whether it's Allah or Jesus, I think it's all bullshit. Men are scum, and they use religion to control women.

All of the women who allow themselves to be abused can keep letting it happen if they choose, but I pass. I've always passed. I've never allowed myself to be on my hands and knees and manipulated. I've been an upstanding and standing up atheist. No man will ever make me kneel down again.

CHAPTER TWO

My Social Worker

The worse beating I ever got was on the day I challenged my father and told him that I wasn't going to kneel down and pray five times a day as the Islamic religion instructs everyone to do.

My brother was mad at me and told on me while we were in the car on the way to our mosque. He told my father that I didn't say my prayers that morning, and, of course, Dad was incensed. He told me to ask Allah for forgiveness in my prayers as soon as I got to the mosque. Then he lectured me on how important it was for me to be a good Muslim, especially since he held such a prominent position in the community. Trust me, whatever he said went in one ear and right out the other.

My father always arrived at the mosque early to have a special prayer with the other early goers and to read over some passages in the Koran. On the day I'm talking about, he had to go to the bathroom really badly and rushed to do a number two prior to joining the other worshippers.

I have to admit, he was in a very cheerful mood that day. I rarely ever remember him being so happy. But he stopped dead

in his tracks when he noticed that I wasn't praying with everyone else.

"You can't shortchange Jah, Aisha," he said. "You must have
a really long prayer with him to be sure he forgives you for your
absentmindedness."

Yeah, my father thought that I'd said a short prayer, and he
was trying to tell me that a rushed prayer wasn't good enough. I
had to have a drawn out one in order for it to be meaningful.

I didn't even have enough time to think about how stupid my
father's thoughts were because my brother ratted on me.

"She didn't even pray yet, Dad," he said.

My father's expression changed into something I'd never seen
before. I knew I was in for it.

Of course, knowing that he was crazy, I tried to smooth things
over. But he didn't even try to hear me. He was, and still is, a
religious fanatic hypocrite.

He pulled me by my long, brittle hair and dragged me to the
altar.

"You will pray to Jah!" he yelled. "You will repent with your
heart and ask for his forgiveness."

I remember feeling like my roots were being cut with razor
blades, it hurt so badly. I'm sure he pulled some of my hair out
that day. The whole shit was so painful and beyond embarrassing.

Maybe the worse part of all, though, was that my father was-
n't alone. He and his other pretend-to-love-God-but-fuck-over-
as-many-women-as-possible cult brothers made a circle around
me and beat me. I think they used thick, crinkly, damaged ropes.
Anyway, as they whipped my skin raw, they shouted, "Pray to
  Pray to Jah!" I swear that was the sickest shit that I've ever

experienced. Now you might think that's a pretty tall tale considering I'd witnessed my mother and her left-side-neck-sucking stupidity. At any rate, I knew that day that I had to get away from that household by all means necessary. I was clueless as to how I would do it, but I knew that I would figure it out.

I remember when I used to go to Rice High School on Lenox. Many of the parents were making a big stink one Saturday at Marcus Garvey Memorial Park because they found out that one of my fellow students was being abused by his parents. The Division of Youth and Family Services (DYFS) didn't step in soon enough to stop it.

There was a big rally at the park, and I remember it seeming like foam was coming out of some of the protesters mouths as they screamed, "If they ain't gonna do their jobs then get them the hell out of there! They have a responsibility to protect our kids."

There is so much passion from all sides when a child is hurt by one of its parents. That day, everyone rallied around the boy, and I felt jealous as hell. My situation caused me pain every single day yet no one helped me. But that's when I figured out what I should do. The next time my father touched me, I would twist and turn myself in such a way so that he would bruise me. Then everyone would know about my dilemma and rally around me just as they did my former classmate.

Sometimes plans seem brilliant when you come up with them. But it's frustrating when they don't work out the way you want them to. I think the Muslims must have a class on how to abuse women without leaving marks or something because no matter how hard I tried to make my father leave bruises when he attacked me, it never happened. I limped away feeling crushed, crumbled and crumpled. But just like Heinz gravy, I had no lumps anywhere. My anticipated freedom from that madman eluded me.

When I feel frustrated, I go to Central Park to look at the weirdos. It's funny, but sometimes looking at other pathetic people relaxes my mind enough to think.

Such was the case when I was walking down Broadway heading to Central Park one day. I was near Columbus Circle about to cross into the park when I saw a man. He was drunk or high or something. Now, I've always thought of Columbus Circle as one of the most dangerous areas for pedestrians. That's why I'm always careful when I go there. Anyway, this man couldn't care less. I doubted he was a heroin addict because he didn't have the leans. But he didn't sway like a drunk either. I knew he was on something because as he crossed the street, he stopped in the middle a couple of times and pointed at God knew what. All the drivers were leaning on their horns, but he continued on his strange way, taking his time until he eventually reached the sidewalk and disappeared.

I thought about him and chuckled as I went to my park bench. I thought of how drunks and crackheads live life without a care in the world. Now, you and I would be worried about what our parents, brothers, sisters or kids—if they were old enough— would do if something happened to us. But in addict's world, he just exists—totally oblivious to the consequences of his actions. That was some deep shit.

I started to wonder if I could live like that. Nah. Even though it would be cool, I remember thinking.

When I finally got the drunk out of my mind, I remembered

why I was at the park in the first place. I needed to figure out how I was gonna piss my father off enough for him to give me bruises.

Sometimes it's hard to concentrate in Manhattan. There's always so much going on. It's too damned busy. I was thinking about my screwed up life but of course was distracted by a punk rock white girl with pink, purple and orange hair. And as if that rainbow weren't enough, she had shaved the sides. She had a gazillion tattoos on her body and at least twenty-five piercings from her eyebrows to her lips and tongue. My father would never let me even get one.

As fascinating as she was, I was distracted by this older white man who was talking on his cell phone. He looked like one of those brainiac types, but his conversation intrigued me.

He was talking about how adolescents always feel misunderstood. He's preaching to the choir, I remember thinking.

Anyway, his words were so powerful to me that I took out my pen and started to write down some of the things he was saying.

My vocabulary at the time wasn't good enough to understand most of what he was talking about but I thought it all probably pertained to me. I was smart enough, though, to write down some of the names of the people he was talking about.

I had been learning the importance of documenting your sources in English class that year so I figured that if I went to the library with the names, it would help me. I ended up being not totally right, but my eavesdropping gave me enough information to make me feel better about my plans.

Of all the names I wrote down, I only found two of them. One guy was named Kehrberg and another one was named McLane.

Interestingly, I was able to find a decent amount of information on both of them.

The Kehrberg dude said that, "Self-mutilating behavior generally begins in adolescence and may be accompanied by distinguishing behaviors."

I wasn't actually sure what he meant, but I'm sure it had something to do with my inflicting pain on myself. Hell, it's not like I'm not hurting enough already when my father does it, I remember thinking. Still, it didn't become totally clear as to what I should do until I read an article by McLane. That's why I used the microfiche to print out his article so I can always remember what he wrote in 1996.

When a subject recalls a painful event from the past, feelings of rejection, anger, shame and low self-worth arise. Previous efforts to communicate this pain have been kept secret due to embarrassment and the unspoken familial code of silence. Pain becomes difficult to communicate and victims use mutilation as a way of expressing overwhelming emotions. Cutting becomes a desperate ploy to obtain empowerment, control and self-healing. After cutting, mutilators feel a sense of calm having found a unique method of organizing the psyche. An all-encompassing pain is ended in one moment allowing the victim a feeling of control.

All I remember thinking after I read that was, I hurt all the time so why not be the one in control if I have to hurt. That's when I started to self-mutilate so I could get bruises. After that, I started calling the New York State Child Abuse and Maltreatment Register (NYSCAMR). I called them so many times I still remember the number. It's 1-800-342-3720, and thankfully for me, especially after I'd done things my father would have kicked my ass for, they were open twenty-four hours a day.

After contacting NYSCAMR several times, I got in a fight with a boy at school for touching my ass. Now, most fathers would back their daughters up after something like that but not mine. All he said was that if I was wearing my Muslim garb so that no one could see my body, it wouldn't have happened.

Speaking of looks, you don't know how I look, so I'll tell you. I'm cute with a body just like the two girls wearing the gold tops in LL Cool J's "Jingling Baby" video. I'm a size seven, but a lot of the time I have to get a size eight or a nine because my butt is too big. My pants are always bunched up at the top because my waist is too small in comparison to my thighs and butt. Anyway, that's why the boy touched it. That's why I cold cocked his ass. And that's why my father was about to tear into my ass because, in his mind, I could have avoided the situation if I'd just done what he told me to do.

To my dismay, the school called my father's pager and left a message. He never wanted them to contact my mother. So there was never any denying what had happened. I was just sitting around, getting sick to my stomach, waiting for him to come home at 5 like he always did. "Our family must always eat together so we can stick together," he always said. But I never felt the love and unity the rest of them had. Especially that day. All I felt was anxiety.

I was never one to run from conflict. I always felt like I might as well get it over with and move on. That's why I was sitting on the couch. I would be the first person my father saw when he walked through the door. But it didn't go down the way I thought it would. I actually lucked out that day.

I heard my father say, "She's not here...she's not here," but I didn't know who he was talking about.

I walked closer to the door so I could better hear what was going on and that's when my father asked, "Do you want to see for yourself that's she's not here?" He opened the door with me and my bruised face standing right on the other side.

"Good try," said the social worker from DYFS whom I later learned was named Sharon as she beckoned to the police.

That was the biggest adrenaline rush I'd ever felt. My nemesis was being taken away. I totally euphoric and safe. My threats were on longer idle. The beauracracy finally came through for me! DYFS was at my house! I knew my father would never be able to harm me again.

ABOUT THE AUTHOR

Sidibe Ibrahima, affectionately called "Sidi", was born and raised in Africa's Ivory Coast. In 1982 he moved to Germany and attended university. There, he developed his entrepreneurial spirit. In 1995, he returned to the Ivory Coast and opened Sidibe & Freres Distribution, an import/export company.

In 2000, able to speak seven different languages and write four, Sidi came to America. He got a job working at a jewelry store for $3.50 an hour and driving a taxicab. As soon as he managed to save $600, he opened his first bookstand in Harlem.

In addition to selling books, Sidi began reading them, many from new publishing companies, and sharing them with other book vendors. With his business savvy and his networking skills, Sidi expanded his business to five bookstands—one in every borough of New York City.

Over the years, Sidi has helped promote many authors—Teri Woods of Teri Woods Publishing, Shannon Holmes of Triple Crown, Danielle Santiago, author of A Little Ghetto Girl in Harlem, and Treasure Blue, author of Harlem Girl Lost to name but a few. On the distribution side, Sidi has assisted Culture Plus and A & B distributors and Say U Promise publication.

Recently, he's worked with Ashante Kahare, author of Homo Thug and has helped his novel to become a bestseller.

Sidi's "start small but think big" attitude has helped him become the most well-known seller of African American books in New York City. He is constantly sent books to review and blueline proofs to approve prior to going to press. Sidi has his finger on the pulse of the African American book patron and a natural instinct for and knowledge of the ever-increasing market for urban literature.

In response to market demand, Sidi has created Harlem Book Center (HBC), a publishing and distribution company based in Harlem. Its first release was *Fatou: An African Girl in Harlem*, a novel Sidi penned himself. Both HBC and "Fatou" are doing extremely well and Sidi expectations have already been surpassed. His hope is to grow HBC into a huge publishing and distribution conglomerate operating both nationally and internationally.

With his natural talents and instincts, Sidi has already accomplished many things in his young life. And his future promises to be exciting and successful. Be sure to visit Harlem Book Center at (www.harlembookcenter.com) or visit him online to keep abreast of current and ongoing projects.

Harlem Book Center
106West 137th Street Ste 5D
New York, NY 10030
Tel: +1/646-739-6166 or +1/646-739-6429